119 LOCUST STREET
GARDEN CITY, NEW YORK 11530

ZELDA THE WELDER

ZELDA BECHT

Copyright © 2013 by Zelda Becht. All rights reserved. No part of this publication may be reproduced, stored in a retrieval system, or transmitted in any form or by any means, electronic, mechanical, photocopying, recording, or otherwise without the prior written permission of the copyright holder, except for brief quotations used in a review.

This is a work of fiction and is produced solely from the author's imagination. People, places, and things mentioned are used in a fictional manner.

ISBN: 978-1492902010
1492902012

Published by moonRox, Inc.
Printed in the United States of America

FOREWORD

The First World War was supposed to end all wars. Twenty years later, it began again, more devious than before. Germany intended to take over the world, one country at a time. Europe was going through hell. England was being bombed daily. And the monster was growing. World War II sped up.

On December 7th, 1941, President Roosevelt announced over the radio,
Japan has attacked Pearl Harbor... a day that will live in infamy.

America was in the fray. We were fighting on two fronts, and we were losing men and ground. Young men were drafted into service every day. Women fought the war in munitions factories, in hospitals, and in shipyards.

I worked at the Kearny Federal Shipyard in New Jersey. We made the best seagoing vessels in the country, and we made them for the best-trained men in the world. We were turning them out as fast as we could, and we were losing them nearly as fast. The tide had to turn soon. The United States had never lost a war. It was our intention we never would.

One third of the shipyard workforce was women. We who welded the ships wore a uniform of sorts, new to us ladies. We bought men's Levi's pants, stiff dark-blue denim. To fit, we nipped in the waist with a belt and rolled up the pant legs as needed. We also wore an impenetrable vest made of heavy suede. A kerchief covered our hair. Though not the most attractive garments, they protected us from the sparks flying from our torches.

We wore an oblong-shaped black shield over our faces held on by a narrow, black metal band circling the head. A strip of dark-tinted glass was built into the shield, enabling us to see while protecting our eyes. When not in use, the protective helmet sat propped atop our head.

Coal-burning barrels were placed throughout the shipyard, keeping us from frostbite. It was the winter of 1943.

Zelda the Welder

CHAPTER ONE

My best friend disappeared the day we were assigned to work together on the top deck of a war ship. No one could tell me where she had gone.

I am Zelda. I weld destroyer escorts at Kearny Federal Shipyard.

In 1943, my country fought in two wars simultaneously, Germany and Japan. The war was going badly. With our men in the service, shipyards were shorthanded. Welders were needed to make the great ships that brought men and supplies to the war. Women were designated to fill the many vacancies. I applied.

I was a legal stenographer for a New York attorney, twenty years old and fresh out of secretarial school. I had never worked near a ship, let alone on one. Working on ships was what *men* did, not girls like me.

I have an unhappy memory of traveling from London to New York on the once magnificent ocean liner, *Leviathan*. I was seasick the entire trip. This would be different, I thought. I wouldn't be sailing on a vessel, just building them. So I attained the necessary release from my current job and heeded my country's call. I said my goodbyes, placed the dustcover over my shiny black Underwood typewriter, and smiled. "I'll be back soon. This war can't last long."

After three days training, I learned how to place rod to holder, spark metal to metal, and create a neat bead, melding two pieces into one. It's called electric arc welding. I was now a welder.

Five days a week, our driver and fellow worker, Jimmy Knapp, drove us girls, Mary, Annie, Janice, and me, from Long Island, New York, to Kearny, New Jersey. It took the better part of two hours each way. My workday started with the alarm clock waking me at five a.m. At six a.m. Jimmy picked us up, and at four-thirty p.m. he drove us home… to eat, sleep, wake, and do it all again.

As we rode, we listened to Jimmy's little battery-driven portable radio. We heard the bands of Jimmy Dorsey, or Benny Goodman, or Artie Shaw. Frank Sinatra sang, or the Andrews Sisters' melodious voices filled the car. We sang along with all the new and great lyrics.

We also heard the news. It wasn't good. Every day we learned of more of our troops being killed or wounded. I prayed the war would end soon, that we could live as we did before that terrible day Japan bombed Pearl Harbor.

We all prayed a lot on those long drives.

On one ride, after seeing the many billboards we passed displaying our proud soldiers and sailors and marines, I turned from the window. "Girls, what do you say we carpool-buddies make a pact? We work on the ships, no matter what, until this rotten war is over and our men are home again."

Faces solemn, they nodded.

I hastily wrote on a slip of paper from my notepad, and we all signed and dated our vow. Leaning forward, I tapped Jimmy on the shoulder. "Do you mind if we put this in the glove compartment? It must remain there until our stint is over."

He looked at me through the rear-view mirror. "I think it's a great idea. I need you girls to help pay for the gas."

That got us laughing, cheering up a serious moment.

For our first six months, we all worked at ground level—but today was to be different. Janice and I would be high up on the top deck of a destroyer escort. To reach it we had to climb a long, skinny ladder braced against the smooth outside of the vessel. Looking straight up, it seemed to go on for miles.

Janice wore a wide grin when we were told our new location. She grabbed my arm. "I can't wait to work on the top of one of those beautiful ships. They are so high, I bet I could touch the sky if I tried." Her eyes danced with delight.

"Yeah," Mary and Annie teased with winks and giggles when we told them. "We know what that's all about. Our handsome foreman, Big Joe Morgan, wants to get you two alone up there."

I laughed along with them, careful not to let them know how edgy I felt.

It wasn't Big Joe that scared me—it was the ship. *I hated heights.* Standing on a chair made me dizzy. I hadn't counted on welding on the *top deck* of a DE. I didn't even like thinking about it. DEs sailed low.

Zelda the Welder

Out of the water, they stood stories tall.

But, I *was* a welder. I did what was required, on the ground or up top. And it helped having a friend like Janice up there with me.

As Jimmy's car neared the shipyard, giant cranes came into view. I decided not to give my new assignment any more thought. Jimmy turned his long, berry-red Buick into the yard's parking lot and edged it into its usual niche. He kept the car spit-polished sparkling. I liked the look of the large, whitewall tires. The convertible top was up on our rides to work, but sometimes, if the weather called for it, he'd put the top down. That was swell.

Today as I stepped out of the car, a blast of freezing wind greeted me. I smelled snow in the air. I rubbed my arms, jumping around to keep warm. "It's going to be a challenge welding in this."

There was a chorus of…

"We're not sissies."

"Think of our boys."

"That's why they pay us so well."

Their brave words were followed by chilly gasps and more arm rubbing as they tried to beat back the wind chill.

At the sign-in clock, the ever-vigilant Otto-the-cop stood guard. He wasn't official police, but we called him that because of his attitude of *Otto is on the job*. He believed it his duty to prevent workers from cheating Federal. He stood, thumbs in pockets, lips drawn into a scowl. His beady little eyes locked on the workers like a hawk on its prey as they slipped timecards into the big, square time clock. He watched them place their cards back in their slots, obviously waiting for someone to do something wrong.

"Good morning, Otto," we sang out as we got in line.

He never, ever returned our happy greetings, just glared at us. "Move on," was his salutation. Sometimes I wondered what was going on inside his head with so many pretty young ladies queued up and nary a smile from him.

I punched the time clock, walked out of the office, and stepped onto the concrete walk. The shipyard was miles and miles long.

Huge cranes laid giant plates of steel on the ground like the pieces of a massive jigsaw puzzle. We welded pieces together and, like waving a magic wand, destroyers and DEs appeared, bobbing gently in their slips. Our country needed ships as fast as we could make them.

I stood on the walk and watched as they launched a DE I had worked on. It slid down the way, elegant and proud, parting the waters with barely a ripple as it glided into the Hackensack River. Soon, it would pick up men and supplies to carry across the Atlantic and Pacific Oceans.

I wanted to shout, *Hey, I helped build her*.

DEs were three hundred feet long. Smaller than the destroyers they protected, they followed behind or sailed alongside the larger ships. They were anti-submarine fighters, ever alert for the enemy. I liked the sense of accomplishment I got as I welded them. Our troops battled on two fronts. With ships like these, we would beat the odds. Nobody messed with the U.S.

As I looked at the vessels Kearny produced, I felt admiration and a sense of wonder. There were all kinds and all sizes.

"I feel so small among these great masses of metal," I said. "These towering ships look like they're impatient to get into the action."

"Sure," Mary said, laughing as she pushed me ahead.

"Sure," Janice said, tightening her pretty scarf, cheeks rosy from the cold. "Let's get to one of the stoves, before I freeze to death."

We greeted the folks standing there, hands held over the hot coals.

The people working at Kearny were primarily women. Some young, like me, who obtained releases from their jobs to build these mighty vessels. And there were older women, moms with kids still in school, giving up their conventional lives to help. They had men overseas—husbands, sons, brothers.

A few men, too, stood warming themselves beside the coal fires. Some had disabilities that prevented them from fighting overseas, but they could contribute here. Others were too old to be drafted, but they were eager to help make the ships. The only requirements were a steady hand and a desire to help.

There was one elderly man. He told us he had closed his small clothing shop for the remainder of the war. "I'd rather use this time helping our boys."

Zelda the Welder

The freezing north wind rocked around us. Shivering, I looked up. The sky had darkened to a sullen gray. The wind blew harder. The river whipped into swells. I smelled the algae and dead fish washed up on the shore, and I rubbed my nose.

It stung at my touch. My face was the only part of me exposed, but multiple layers of clothing hadn't kept the chill from penetrating to my bones. It's this darn weather, I thought. The wide-open spaces invited the bitter wind to race between the tall ships. It was winter's song—whistling, piercing, screeching sounds sending chilling shivers up my spine.

"Thank heavens for the coal fires," I said. "They're the only relief from this blasted cold. This smelly black smoke might get onto everything I wear, but I relish the warmth." I held my gloved hands over the fire and glanced at Janice. "It will be worse at the top."

She nodded, pointing to the vessel she and I were to work on today. The ladder resting against its side seemed like miles and miles of spaghetti-thin grey metal. It went straight up, never ending, nothing but air between it and the hard, hard ground below.

I grimaced. *How was I to climb that?*

We couldn't waste any more time. I could almost hear Big Joe yelling. Janice and I picked up our rod-filled buckets. With a sigh, I pushed away from the warmth.

Time for my trip to the top of the world.

Abruptly, Janice veered away.

"Where are you going?" I called. "Remember, Big Joe said we can't be late."

"It's going to be really windy up there." She wrapped her bit of leopard silk tighter around her neck, tucking it into her fleece-lined jacket. "This won't be enough. I have a woolen sweater in my locker."

"I'll wait for you."

"No, I'll just be a minute," Janice said. "You go on ahead."

"Oh, okay."

I tried to sound cheerful, but I had expected to have Janice climb with me. So despite what she'd said, or in spite of it, I stopped at a glowing coal stove to wait for her, reluctant to leave its warmth, to go up on my own.

The high-cuffed, suede welding gloves designed to ride halfway up our arms were worn as protection from sparks flying from our torches. Mine had several scorch marks to prove it, and a singed stench greeted me when I nosed too close. Today, the chill found its way into the open tops of my gloves, and I yanked them off to rub my hands above the red-hot coals. I glanced at my watch. Ten minutes had passed. Still no Janice.

What could she be doing? It's eight-thirty.

I pulled on my gloves. "Stop this nonsense, Zelda," I mumbled. "You're not a baby. You can do whatever Janice can do."

A welder nearby glanced up and grinned as she bent to rub her hands over the fire. I smiled back, feeling foolish. I was acting like a scared kid.

Several feet away, Mary and Annie were warming themselves at another barrel.

"Is Janice with you?" I called from my tin-can stove.

They waved, shaking their heads. "Not here," Mary called back.

She's gone up without me. Damn. Wait until I get my hands on her.

CHAPTER TWO

The formidable, foldable ladder still leaned against one side of the bulkhead, waiting. It could be moved to other locations as needed, or, it occurred to me, could as easily be toppled by a sudden strong wind. And a mighty long fall it would be.

I must stop thinking negatively. The ladder was my only means of boarding the ship, short of sprouting wings or dropping down from an airplane.

Slipping my face-shield's black band against my forehead, I flipped the shield up, balancing it atop my head until needed. When welding, I would bring it down to peer through its narrow, glass window.

I walked to the ladder. Torches lay on the ground, connected to an electrical box nearby. Suede gloves on, I reached for one. While plugged into the power on the ground, said torch would travel with me as I high as I had to go. With my bucket of rods also in hand, I gathered my nerve, ready to begin the next phase of my life. Allowing I had one after this. A prayer seemed appropriate. I would take all the help I could bargain for.

Standing in front of the mountain of smooth gray, I looked up. Gritting my teeth, I determined this inane, insane fear would not master me. After all, hundreds of other brave souls had climbed before me.

Reaching with my left hand, I took a deep breath, slowly let it out, and stepped on the first rung. I allowed my imagination to lead. With each step, I fancied my boot pressing down on Big Joe's handsome, grinning face, the grin he used when he told us where we would be working today. I leaned in, resting my body against the ladder for support. Again, raising a booted foot, I grasped the next rung, then brought up the other. There was Big Joe's face. Stomping hard on each rung made the ascent easier.

Finally, after what seemed forever, I reached what would be, when completed, the upper deck of a DE. I took a tentative look down. A mistake. I swallowed the lump in my throat, leaned in, and squeezed the upper rung with my one free hand. I gave another tug on the electric cord and pulled myself over the top and onto a steel plate. I felt comforted as I stood firmly on solid steel once again. This wasn't so bad.

The wind blew stronger up here, colder but clearer. I had a moment's flash of the cozy office I had left to work at Federal, but quickly erased it. We who made ships would not let weather deter us. I chuckled, and my heart's excessive beating quieted. I searched the deck. Janice would appreciate my story.

Where the dickens was she?

A temporary wooden shed stood along one side. I guessed the small building was to store tools and the like. Perhaps even a toilet. A short distance from it lay metal plates, a large section ready and waiting to be welded together. I had expected to see Janice kneeling there, already at work.

Standing at the bow, I glanced down the incredible length of the deck. Nearby, several workers bent over large pieces of paper laid out on the steel. They appeared to be working on a blueprint. They spoke with loud, questioning voices and pencils in hand. Some held coffee cups. I wondered where I might get some.

I started toward them. "Janice? You there?" I called.

Glancing my way, a man waved, then answered, "Not here," and returned to the project.

So, where was the girl?

As I watched, a tall man moved from the group, heavy boots clomping loud on the laid-out steel. He got closer. It was Big Joe Morgan. As the name implied, he was a big man, muscular, handsome in a rough, outdoorsy way. Dark, curly hair showed from the sides of his steel hat.

He grinned, white teeth sparkling in the winter sun, dark eyes piercing mine, voice accusatory. "Zelda. I expected you earlier." Then he grinned again. "How was the trip up?"

I would have hit him with the bucket of rods, but I restrained myself. I daren't damage such a perfect example of narcissistic manhood. "Just fine, Mr. Morgan. No problem at all." I indicated the area around us where metal abutted metal not yet joined by weld. "You want me to start, or should I wait for Janice?"

He pointed to a section of the pre-laid steel plates. "Maybe we can get this end finished by quitting time," he said, his voice more a command than an inquiry.

"But wasn't Janice supposed to be working here, too?"

He paused. A look of alarm crossed his face, but it was there and gone so quickly, I decided I imagined it. "Janice? She'll be along shortly. Ran an errand for me. Start working. You *will* get it done on time." Big Joe nodded toward the plates to be joined and turned away.

Nasty man.

The ladder remained empty. Janice's absence was disappointing, but there was nothing I could do about it. The sooner I got to work, the sooner I could leave.

Placing a rod in my holder, I walked to the first sheet and examined the layout. The area was large. The massive steel plates lying side by side would eventually be one expansive deck. My imagination flowed. I pictured sailors in white Navy uniforms strolling the lovely ship *I* helped build. I did feel satisfaction in being part of a vessel our service men would sail on.

Kneeling on one knee, my shield over my face, I hit the rod to the spot. My arc sparked, the metal melting as I swung an eighth of an inch forward, a sixteenth of an inch back. Forward, back, forward, back in a gentle motion, sparks flying like tiny fireworks. The melted metal hardened into a neat, rippling seam, and the smaller sheets of steel grew into one.

The gaseous smell of ozone floated in the air around me, fumes made by my sparking torch and the melting metal, but it was less pronounced up here in the open. Working up top had its compensations. If only I could get warm.

I had one last strip to finish. I pulled off my glove to glance at my watch. Eleven-thirty. Three hours passed since I climbed the ladder. The morning had moved along. It was almost noon and still no Janice. With only a small section left, I intended to finish the stretch, and then I would look for her. I had to know where Big Joe sent my friend.

Almost at the end of the strip, I stopped to inspect what I'd done. With my metal-bristled brush, I swept the bond clean. I was pleased. The weld was evenly spaced and running like a lovely row of knitting. I always tried to make my work neat, the bead straight, near perfect.

This was the narrowest part of the ship. I hoped I had enough rods to finish the line. I turned to glance behind me. Just off my path lay a large, off-white duffle bag. Its contents bulged. It leaned lopsidedly.

That wasn't there before. Wonder what's in it?

Putting my torch down, I stood, stretching to get the kinks out. It felt good to stand after kneeling for so long. I sauntered to the duffle bag, studied it, and pushed it with my foot. It was a lot heavier than it looked.

Bending, I pulled at the strings to see inside, then stopped at a rustle above me. Big Joe stood there. He reached for the bag, effortlessly moving it a distance away from the panel I was working on. With a shrug, I knelt to finish the several feet of welding I had left.

Suddenly, his boots were in my way.

I stared up at him. "Bag looked heavy."

"Just dirty clothes. I dropped it there to close the shed. Didn't mean to disturb you. Listen, it's almost lunchtime. Why not break now?"

I glanced where I thought Big Joe had moved the bundle, hoping it wouldn't be in my way again. It wasn't anywhere in sight. That was when the cold feeling wrapped around me and wouldn't leave. Something was wrong—but I couldn't say what.

I forced myself to be calm. Turning back, I found myself looking up into Big Joe's dark eyes. Searching for the right words, not finding any, I simply blurted, "Joe, where *is* Janice? Why isn't she up here working with me?"

He stared me down. "What are you talking about?"

I swallowed, tried again. "Janice was supposed to work with me today. She was so excited to work up here halfway to the sky. But she isn't here. Where is she?"

"Zelda, get it together. I needed her someplace else. Drop it."

Everything was building—Janice, the ladder, the bundle, my imagination. My teeth bit down on my lip. My mind whirled. *Okay, Mr. Morgan. As soon as I finish this strip, I'm going down. I may not come up again.*

He was leaning over me when I hit my rod to the metal and let the sparks fly where they may—I hoped into his eyes. I wanted to hurt him. I didn't give a damn what he thought. I was dead angry. He wasn't telling me everything. I knew it and he knew I knew it.

By twelve o'clock, I had completed the section, packed my gear, and made for the ladder. With the line slung over my shoulder and my free hand grasping the side rail, I gingerly put one booted foot over the edge and onto the top rung. Sliding one rung at a time, I worked my way down. Once on the ground, I leaned against the ladder, breathing quietly, calming myself. I gazed up the side of the gray behemoth.

Big Joe was gone.

CHAPTER THREE

Someone called my name, and I turned. Big Joe stood behind me, grinning from ear to ear like Alice's Cheshire Cat.

Where the devil did he come from?

"Planning to work this afternoon?" he asked. "Or would you rather sit it out the next four hours?"

"You're too good to me. Thanks, Mr. Morgan, but after lunch, I have a job to finish. Remember the troops."

He grinned again. "You're working down here this afternoon."

He was playing with me—with that same stupid grin. I stared at him.

His expression turned serious. "I don't want you to go up again today. There's work to be done down here. Max will show you. When you get home tonight, you should take it easy. Tomorrow you work the whole day up top. And no complaints."

I said, "And will Janice be back on the job tomorrow?"

"I expect so." He turned and walked away.

I spent the rest of the day welding at ground level while my mind drifted between my missing friend and Big Joe's vague answers. If I had to work up top tomorrow, I could look forward to stomping on his face all the way up. That would satisfy me. There was something not quite kosher about his attitude, like he didn't want me to know where Janice was working. What could he have her doing?

I thought of Big Joe Morgan's dark eyes, always seeming to hold a smile. A smile? It seemed more like a leer. Besides being good-looking, he looked healthy and strong. So why wasn't he in the service like most of the able-bodied men—like my friends, like my neighbor Ida's son? How did *he* get out of it?

At the end of the day, I walked to the car. The girls were already seated.

"Where's Janice?" I asked.

Jimmy piped up. "She left a note on the car. She won't be driving home with us tonight. Got a lift with someone else."

I stared at him, at the girls, and at him again. Slowly, I got into the car. No one said any more about our missing friend. No one seemed to think her absence strange.

On the drive home, my mind raced with thoughts and questions. *This was not like her. Not like her at all. Damn her, how could she do this to us? To me? She had never done this before. None of us had ever gone home with someone else. What had happened since she left me this morning?*

Jimmy dropped me off at my home. I smiled and waved goodnight, but I was troubled. Janice wouldn't stick a note on Jimmy's car—she would speak to one of us. I had been prepared to let her know I was angry. I swallowed my annoyance, replacing it with worry.

There was no moon, and it was dark on the street as I unlocked my door. When Meow, my black and white tabby, greeted me, brushing his warm body against my leg, it was comforting, easing my black mood some. Not interested in dinner, I made a cheese sandwich and a glass of milk. I ate the simple meal, washed the one dish and glass, let them drain dry, and went to my bedroom.

It was close to eight o'clock, still too early to go to bed and too late to do anything else. But perhaps I should do as Big Joe suggested and get some rest. It had been a troubling day. Whatever tomorrow brought, I needed to be ready for it.

Yawning, I wound my small alarm clock for the morning. I scratched my head vigorously, ran my fingers through my long hair, then brushed it very hard. Tied up in a bandana all day, it needed stimulation. This always relaxed me, made me ready for sleep.

Only it wasn't working this time. I lay down, stretched my body, worked at unwinding, and pounded my pillow to get comfortable. I wanted to sleep, wanted to push the growing concern away. Nothing succeeded tonight.

Get to sleep, Zelly. Shut down those thoughts rattling around your cranium. It's taking you nowhere. Sleep.

She'll come to work tomorrow with a perfectly plausible explanation. I'll feel like a total idiot.

And if she doesn't show? But why wouldn't she?

The men working on top with me claimed they hadn't seen her. I believed them. I would find out if someone on the ground had seen Janice after she left the locker room, and who was with her.

Over and over, one thought repeated itself. *It was not like her not to tell me where she went.*

Janice and I had been best friends since grade school. She was slender, and taller than me by three inches. Her long red hair and laughing blue eyes drew admiring looks her way. I remembered how when she was kidding around, her eyes flashed like she was thinking of something devilish. And the fun times we spent lately—dancing with the GIs at Clinton Hall, the movies at the Maspeth Theater.

I was there when her little boy was born. Her husband, Bill, was overseas, RAF, in England. His plane went down over the Atlantic. After that, Janice became withdrawn for a while. But I understood, supported her, got her to sign up at Federal and become a welder like me.

Suddenly I remembered. Good grief. Her little boy, Billy. Janice's mother, Sadie, always watched him while Janice was at work. I would call Sadie first thing in the morning. Perhaps she would know… Know what? Sadie couldn't know where Janice worked today. And what would I tell her and little Billy? That we had expected to work on a ship together? That she was excited at the prospect of working directly on a real deck, only she never showed?

No, I couldn't call Janice's home. I was making too much of the whole thing. In the morning, Janice would look at me like I was some kind of a loon.

Big Joe said he'd given her another job. Where could she be working that she had to put a note on the car saying she wouldn't be riding home with us? Okay, she was flighty lately, but what would make her just leave a note?

With my eyes wide open, I stared at the ceiling, exhausted yet unable to doze off. I heard every creak as the night crawled on.

So it came as a shock when the alarm clock rang on the nightstand. Meow jumped down from my headboard onto my pillow, vocally adding to the bedlam. *It's time to rise and greet the new day,* the cat purred.

I barely missed the fleeing cat as my arm swept out from the beneath my quilt to stop the ringing. I strained to read the small black numbers while grasping for the tiny lever to shut the blame thing off. My finger caught under one of the two small bells making the racket.

"Ouch," I yelped, ready to throw the pretty little clock against the wall. The Baby Ben was a gift, though at that moment, I could be persuaded to return it to its maker, Westclox.

"Sheesh, it's freezing in here," I said to the empty room. Still holding the silenced timepiece, I slipped my chilled arm once more beneath the eiderdown. The feather quilt was a gift from my English mother, and I loved its warmth.

I must have dozed again. I woke with my cheek being nuzzled by Meow who was sprawled atop me and mewing softly. In Meow talk, he was saying, *I'm hungry, girl. Please get up and fix my breakfast.* His whiskers tickled my nose and I sneezed. Slowly opening one eye, then the other, I brought the clock out from under the covers, squinting to read the time.

"Good God, I'm late," I shouted, placing the accursed timepiece back on my nightstand.

I threw the bedclothes aside, sending Meow flying off the bed. Jimmy would be outside my door in half an hour. Janice had better be there. And she better have a good story. Lowering my legs to the floor, I made for the bathroom. I had to shower and dress. There were chores to tend to, a cat to feed, a girlfriend to scold, a mystery to resolve. And Big Joe had me working three stories up atop an unfinished DE.

Clutching my robe, I retrieved the bottle of milk that was left on the front stoop by Barney, my milkman. I poured the cream at the top into a small pitcher. That went into the icebox. Some milk from the bottle went into Meow's dish.

I glanced at the big red-apple clock hanging on the kitchen wall. A wooden worm sporting a top hat and cane protruded from its side. I loved that clock, but this morning my thoughts were of the minutes ticking away, not the decoration.

There wasn't time to empty the water under the icebox. I'd been too upset last night to think of it. I hoped it would wait until this evening and not flood my floor.

By six o'clock, I had showered, dressed, downed two cups of coffee, and ate a slice of wheat toast—lightly buttered and smeared with a dot of orange marmalade. In my lunch box, I threw a cheese sandwich wrapped in waxed paper and a thermos filled with the remaining coffee.

For work, I wore *Levis 501 Jeans,* pants made of a tightly woven material called denim, perfect for welding in nasty-cold or super-hot shipyards. They had rivets at the corners of the pockets and the bottom of the button fly, increasing the wear. And they were heavy enough to deflect the sparks created by my torch. Made in San Francisco, the pants were designed for men—construction workers, railway workers, loggers, and the like. I'd bought the smallest size available and rolled up each pant leg. I pulled the waist tight with a belt. There must be some mighty slight men out there, because the fit was not all that bad for my five-foot-two, one-hundred-and-three pound frame. I also wore my black, wool-lined pea coat. It was light, but warm.

Meow sat on the front windowsill watching me, unblinking, a wise gleam in his sphinxlike green eyes.

I wondered what mischief he would dream up as soon as he was alone. I no longer hung lace curtains at the windows with Meow perched there as my sentinel. Even clipped, his claws had done a right job on them. Since it took so much time and trouble drying the fabric on the wooden rack, stretching the material just so, hooking the ends to those hundreds of nails, I had given up on them. When the choice was the curtains or Meow, my pet won. A white pull-shade had to do. It wasn't as pretty as lace curtains, but Meow was.

    I rushed out the door then waved to my kitty as Jimmy tooted the horn.

CHAPTER FOUR

I locked my front door and walked to the car, glancing across the street. Ida was washing her steps. She was my neighbor, a motherly Polish lady. The front of her house had three narrow, side-by-side windows. In the middle window, hanging by a gold cord, was a patch of white silk about six-inches by six-inches. It had a gold star sewn in the center, signifying that a family member died in the war.

Most of yesterday's snow had melted, and Ida was bent over, scrubbing away at her brick stoop. Her housedress billowed behind her. She finished the bottom step, and the wet gleamed in the morning sun. She scrubbed a lot since she received notice that her son, Peter, had been killed in Africa. There were hundreds and hundreds of such losses. The papers were full of news from overseas. I understood her pain. I knew a number of GIs who had been killed or wounded. This was her child who was gone.

Since the beginning of the war, we were rationed on many items, sugar being one. After her son was killed, Ida developed a peculiar craving for the sweet stuff. She ate it by the handful, running out of her monthly allotment early. I and several of our neighbors gave her a cupful at a time from our own rations. Perhaps it eased her unhappiness. I only hoped that with time she wouldn't feel the need.

Ida looked up from across the road, and I called, "See you this evening, Ida. I have something for you." She nodded and waved back.

Annie was in the front seat next to Jimmy. She greeted me with a smile.

I bounced in beside Mary, sitting in back. "No Janice?"

"I haven't heard from her," Mary said.

Annie looked around at me and shook her head. "Me, neither."

"Jimmy, did she call? Did she tell you anything?"

He glanced at me in his rearview mirror. "Nope. I honked at her door, but she didn't come out. I thought you might have heard from her."

Zelda the Welder

"Where do you think she went?" I asked Mary.

Instead of answering, she gazed out the window at some soldiers walking down the street. She grinned at them and blew a kiss. "They might be more fun than working on some dumb boats."

I knew she was only teasing. Mary was a flirt, but that was as far as it went.

She turned, patting my knee. "You know, you really should stop worrying about her. She's a big girl. If she wants to mess around, that's her choice."

I stared at her. "This is serious. It's going into the second day. She certainly would have told someone if she intended *not* to ride with us. Besides, she was supposed to work with me."

Annie reached back to take my hand. "Look, why don't you call her mother? Surely, she'll know something. And you'll feel better."

"Sure." I turned and looked out the window. Nobody else seemed to care. Was it just me? Even Big Joe acted like I was some kind of a fool. I was overreacting. I'll give her just one more day, before I call her house. If Sadie doesn't know, I'll call the police. Yes, that's what I'll do. I felt better with a plan and tried to relax.

Mary and Annie gabbed on about Mary's birthday tomorrow. We all planned to see Frank Sinatra sing at a matinee at the *Paramount Theatre*. The discussion was where to eat dinner afterwards.

Mary said, "Let's just have some White Castle cheeseburgers. That will give us time to get to Clinton Hall and dance with the soldiers. Cheering them up is a worthy cause."

"That's my Mary. Miss Goodwill Flirt of 1943," I mumbled under my breath.

"Did you say something?" she asked.

I shook my head and kept silent for the rest of the ride. In my mind, I reran what happened the day before. I had expected Janice to be in the car. I thought she would straighten out the muddle of yesterday. There must be a simple explanation. She couldn't just not show. That only happened in Agatha Christy novels.

We were early reaching the Yard. The wind blew hard. The chilling blasts of icy air tore around the docked ships, rocking them with creaks and moans where they sat on the ways.

Zelda the Welder

After we clocked in, Mary said, "Zelda, come with us. Warm up by the fire before starting."

I shook my head. "Love to, but if I'm on top deck again, I want to get a hot coffee first." I waved to the girls, then pulled my woolen scarf tighter around my neck as I faced into the wind. I would put my things away then head for the cafeteria.

I reached my locker and stopped. The door was wide open. My suede vest lay crumpled on the bottom, half in and half out. *It must have slipped off its hook. What was I thinking? Was I so distraught yesterday I'd neglected to close and lock the door?* At least I had nothing of real value inside—just my vest and a sweater.

Today was one of those days an extra sweater was welcome, and I was glad it was there. It would help in this blasted cold. I slipped it on, then the vest over it, rubbing my hands down the suede to smooth out the wrinkles. A glance in the small mirror on my door told me I wasn't finished. After I redid my lipstick, I wrapped a red cotton bandana around my head. It and the shield protected me from the sparks my rod made. The lipstick was for another cause.

Just because we girls welded was no reason to ignore our femininity.

Finished with the refurbishing, I put my purse and coat inside. This time I made sure I closed the door and spun the lock before leaving.

Our vests didn't have pockets, but I had sewn one on the inside of mine. I always carried a few cents to get a drink or a snack during the day, and it was easier to get at loose change there than from the small, slit-like pockets in my Levi's. In the cafeteria, I slid my hand in to pay for my coffee and touched something. I pulled a scrap of lined notepad paper from my pocket and slowly turned it over in my hands. It was folded several times.

How did that get in there?

I paid for my coffee and walked to a table. There, I unfolded the note and spread it out. I read the words, then read them again, shaking my head in disbelief. It was a message, but it wasn't written by hand. Pieces of cut and pasted newsprint spelled out:

your FRIEND is on VACATION in Miami

I stared, lips pursed, suppressing a laugh. This had to be a joke—a nasty one, but a joke nonetheless. I glanced around the cafeteria. No one appeared to be showing an interest in me. I'd expected someone to be smiling, watching their little joke play out. Who had put this in my pocket? Could anyone really believe I would accept this as true? What were they trying to say? When had they put it there? Last night? Early this morning?

Realization hit me. *Someone broke into my locker. I* hadn't *forgotten to lock it.*

Suddenly, it wasn't funny. I was damned angry. I turned at a sound behind me.

Big Joe stood grinning down at me. He pointed to the door. "Hey, the job awaits. Lots of work to do. The boys need their ships."

He sounded like one of those poster billboards plastered on the highway. I guessed he hoped to appear chummy, but while he spoke his dark eyes darted back and forth from my face to the note in my hand. It did look odd, pieces of newsprint stuck on a sheet of paper. I folded it and placed it in my vest pocket. I wasn't ready to discuss the contents. I wanted to know how it got there, but this wasn't the time.

I gave him as big a grin as I could and stood. "Is Janice on board today?"

His voice softened as he rested his arm across my shoulder. "Zelda, we have a deadline. You must stop worrying about Miss Bates and go build a ship."

I got a squirmy feeling at his touch. Shivers danced up my spine. I always judged people by their eyes, and there was something in Big Joe's eyes I couldn't read.

Backing away, I picked up my gear. "Right. I'm on my way."

I left the cafeteria at a fast trot, heading for the office across the lot. There was a telephone there, and I intended to contact the police and report Janice missing. At the door, I glanced back. Big Joe stood leaning in the cafeteria doorway, arms folded, his black hair gleaming in the early morning light. He was watching me, his gaze intent.

CHAPTER FIVE

The offices of the Kearny Federal Shipyard were staffed with one secretary and one clerk, plus the boss man himself, Mr. Fen Hansen. The large outer office bustled with people, loud voices talking and laughing.

Most of the noise came from a group of men clustered at a table. They were organizing a launch, the christening of a new destroyer, and they expected to have several distinguished guests. I realized it wasn't a good time to have the police milling about asking questions.

That must be why Big Joe was so put off by my questions. Perhaps he didn't want anything to disrupt the festivities. I decided to speak to Mr. Hansen before calling the police. After all, Janice was missing from *his* shipyard.

Through his office window, I saw Mr. Hansen sitting at his desk. He was a short man but large in girth, and he looked even larger in his double-breasted suit. I could see the pull of his buttoned jacket across his ballooning chest. Food rationing didn't hamper his consumption, I surmised.

I walked to the secretary sitting at the desk outside his office. She looked to be about twenty-five. Her nameplate read *Silvia Stern*. I had never met her. She wore her dark hair in a sleek upswept hairdo and a tailored black suit with a white collared blouse. Looking very chic, indeed. I liked the new styles they were showing—the wide shoulders and shorter skirts. Something I would have worn if I were still working in New York for Miller, Esq. Standing in front of her, I felt shabby in men's Levi's and scorched vest, with my hair wrapped in a red bandana. But I had no regrets. I was doing what felt right and honorable, working on great American warships.

Miss Stern looked up from her black Smith-Corona typewriter and smiled. A dimple cut a crease in one cheek, bringing me back to the reason I was there—Janice.

"I'd like to have a word with Mr. Hansen," I said. "It *is* important that I see him this morning."

Her voice chipper, she said, "I'm sorry. You'll have to wait. Give me your name and have a seat." She pointed with a red-lacquered fingernail to an empty chair.

Obviously, I didn't impress her. I guessed *Zelda the Welder* was not all that outstanding in the scheme of shipyards. There was nothing to do but sit in the chair she indicated and wait.

I glanced around, wishing I could get it over with and leave. I had work waiting. The table near me held an array of women's magazines, catering to the majority of workers in the Yard—*Better Homes and Gardens, Good Housekeeping, McCall's, Redbook, The Ladies Home Journal*. But I was jittery being there, too tense to read.

The door to the Yard opened, and Big Joe came in. My stomach plummeted. With a nod and a warm smile, Miss Stern ushered him into Mr. Hansen's inner-sanctum.

As he walked into Hansen's office, I grabbed a *Ladies Home Journal* to hide behind. I peeked over the top. Through the window in Mr. Hansen's office, I saw Big Joe gesturing, his hands flying as he spoke. I wished I could hear what he said. Perhaps it was about Janice, or perhaps me. Hansen nodded several times. Pretty soon they shook hands, and Big Joe left. He didn't look my way, yet he must have known I was there—he'd watched me enter the office from the cafeteria.

Before I had a chance to consider what I'd seen, however, Miss Stern stood and beckoned. I laid down the magazine and went into the office.

Mr. Hansen didn't look up when I entered. He was sitting in his chair. Crammed into it would be a better description. I felt dwarfed standing in front of the overstuffed man. I cleared my throat.

He continued reading the page in front of him.

I coughed into my hand lightly, then more vigorously.

Still he gave no recognition that anyone was in the room.

Heaving a deep sigh, I said, "Mr. Hansen?"

He raised his head, his chin pointing my way. His glasses were framed in gold, and he stared through the huge round rims, his eyes magnified. He was near-sighted all right, as in only-see-what-you-want-to-see, which might account for what followed. "Miss Bea, is it? Have a seat, please. I'll be with you in a minute." He went back to what he was reading. After a time, he signed the paper, set it aside, neatly placed his pen beside the document, and only then looked at me. He curled his lips and exposed his teeth in what looked like as phony a grin as they came. "Now, what is this about a missing person?"

"Mr. Hansen, you already seem to know why I am here. Perhaps I should begin at the beginning."

He waved for me to go on, then held up his chin with clasped hands. His eyelids drooped in boredom or weariness or both.

I mentally grit my teeth, took a deep breath, and began. "Yesterday, I worked on the top deck of a DE bulkhead. Slip thirteen. A fellow welder, Janice Bates, was assigned to work with me. I looked for her, but she never showed."

Hansen's portly body shifted forward, his chair squeaking as he leaned over his desk. His eyes squinted as he stared at me. "Why is it so important that you work with this particular woman?"

His question took me off guard. I gulped. "That isn't the issue. We received our assignment together. We talked about it while car-pooling to the Yard. Yesterday morning, she went back to her locker for a sweater. I haven't seen her since. I asked around. No one else has seen her."

I waited for his reaction. There was none.

"You did hear me, didn't you, Mr. Hansen? She is gone. She did not ride home with us yesterday. She did not ride in with us today. S*he has disappeared. We don't know where she is*." My voice had grown louder. It was almost a shout. I stopped. This wouldn't do. I must remain calm.

Hansen stared at me. "So you say." Sunlight glared from the window behind him, striking his thin gray hair, highlighting his prominent nose.

If his arrogant lack of interest was intended to frustrate me, it was succeeding. I stood, prepared to leave, then stopped. I must try one more time. "Mr. Hansen, my friend is missing... gone... no one knows where... yesterday... from Kearny. Isn't it customary for the police to be made aware? Has anyone notified the police?"

"Please, young lady, sit." He pushed his body up, waddled around the desk, and stopped beside my chair. I shuddered as he took my small hand in both his large, moist ones. His expression changed from stern to benevolent.

"I do understand how you feel. But your friend is a grown woman. Where she goes is her business. After all, it is only one day."

I pulled my hand away, whispering, "Joe Morgan has already filled you in."

He heard and blanched.

Before he could say another word, I stood and walked out his door, past his well-dressed secretary, and fled the building.

What was the point? Until I found some proof, no one was going to believe me, not even the police. Meanwhile, the ships had to be made. I had my assignment.

I hesitated only a moment before climbing the ladder that had haunted me the day before. I had no time to be afraid. I would go up today because I had to. I would be working alone.

As I climbed, Janice filled my head. My thoughts whirled. I had a flash—Big Joe on the deck as I was leaving—a minds-eye view of the shed behind him. Where would anyone go who didn't want to be seen? The shed. Perhaps Janice had shown up at the top of the DE after all. Perhaps she went into the shed, maybe looking for me, and someone had been hiding there.

And did what? Such silliness. This was altogether too much like an Agatha Christy mystery.

Before I realized it, I reached the top. I stepped on the deck. To my right was the mysterious shed. I put down my gear and walked to its small, wooden door. What would it hurt if I went in? I reached for the doorknob and turned it. The door swung open, surprising me. I had expected it to be locked. I stared at the door. Okay, so it opened. I might as well check it out. I peered inside. There were no windows to break the darkness, but a band of light came in through the open doorway sufficient to show a bare light bulb. I pulled the cord, and a yellow glow filled the area.

Taped boxes stood stacked against all four walls. In one corner, several boxes were askew as though they had been pushed out of place. Drops of something dark trailed over a section of the floor. They led to the doorway, ending where I stood. I took out my handkerchief and rubbed at several of the larger spots, collecting what residue I could. It was the color of faded rust. Or dried blood?

It could be Janice's, my overworked imagination screamed. Carefully, I folded the cloth, then placed it in my vest pocket to be studied later. I had seen the police do that many times in movies. The local police might be able to tell something from what I had salvaged.

I turned for a last glance. The light caught a small wastebasket tucked in the corner. I reached in. Just some rumpled newspapers. I tossed them back. Taking one last look around, I pulled the light cord and closed the door behind me. The shed held no empty corners large enough for a body. Gruesome thought. Still, as I left, something nagged at me. Like I had missed a clue.

I tossed aside all errant thoughts. I was intent on finishing my welding in spite of the clouding sky. I noticed occasional flurries and hoped it would stay light until the larger plates were completed. They had been laid out from one end of my section of the deck to the other, huge, long, rectangular sheets of metal that could only be lifted by the mammoth cranes dotting the shipyard. I was expected to finish this project today.

I worked without stopping for the next few hours. The flurries had ended. They had been a sample of what was to come, I was sure. Allowing myself a ten-minute break to eat the lunch I'd brought from home, I found a corner shielded from the wind. It felt pleasant where I sat, peaceful really, up so high and alone. I thought of the GIs away in the war. Maybe the work I did would help them get home sooner. It was a nice thought.

As I put my sandwich wrapper back in my box, I glanced beyond the edge of the deck and looked down to the yard below. I picked out Mary and Annie standing by a coal fire with some of the other girls. I called, and they waved.

"Send up some of that heat," I yelled.

They made silly gestures, pushing up empty air, but it didn't get any warmer where I stood. I settled for blowing into my hands.

From this high, nothing broke the spectacular view beyond the masts and cranes littering the yard. In both directions, shipways held either completed or waiting to be completed vessels—destroyers, destroyer escorts, cargo ships. I read in *The Halyard* that this yard had 750 miles of docks and over a hundred slips. Today only a few of the slips appeared full. We had our work waiting. When one vessel launched, another keel was set in its place.

In the distance, behind the people milling about, the Hackensack River stretched out. Streaks of sun reflected on the water, and small ribbons of silver rippled in the wind.

This is where they sail from, the mighty ships we make.

The flurries began again, this time in earnest. The deck soon looked like it was painted white. I could brush aside only so much moisture. If it got any worse, I would have to go down. And if Mr. Hansen hadn't notified the police by then, I intended to call them myself.

I worked until the whistle blew at four o'clock, but the police did not come to ask me about Janice. I knew what I had to do.

With studied caution, I swung over the edge, my jaw clenched. Again, I carried my torch and bucket in one hand while I grasped the ladder with the other. The snow made the ladder slippery. I pressed flat against the skinny metal. It was like trying not slide down a wet chute. My fingers stung as I hung on. I tapped my steel-tipped black boots hard against each rung. Then I was down. Both feet hit solid ground, and I opened my eyes. Slowly, I released my fingers and pushed away from the ladder. I let out a deep-held breath. There had to be a better way.

The shipyard hummed with voices as guys and gals clustered around a canned fire. I extended my near-frozen fingers and felt the exquisite pain of warmth. I didn't move for several minutes, enjoying the wisecracks and sheer fun of hanging out with the others.

But the back of my mind still gnawed at the problem. I would ask Jimmy to stop at the police station to report Janice missing.

CHAPTER SIX

I beckoned to the girls, and we went to look for our driver.

When we reached Jimmy Knapp in the parking lot, he had just finished dusting snow off his pride and was folding the clean cloth. He cared for that car like it was his first-born. Its wide, whitewall tires stood out against a chrome bumper so shiny one could almost read the newspaper in its mirror-like finish.

"Jimmy," I said, "would it be out of the way to stop at the police station before we left town? I want to report Janice missing. Maybe I can get through to them better in person than over the telephone."

"Why not? If it will make you feel better. I've been wondering why she never called me to say she wouldn't be riding with us today. She should have let one of us know. Unless, of course, she was tied up." He laughed, raising his arm to deflect my poorly aimed swing.

"That was a terrible thing to say."

"I didn't mean it that way. Gosh, you really are worried about her. Okay, we'll stop at the stationhouse."

"Swell. Thanks. It shouldn't take long."

Jimmy was a good guy. We were grateful he wasn't in the service, that he could drive us to Jersey every day. Since the war started, young men without children were drafted. Jimmy wasn't drafted because he was over thirty, had a family, and worked at Kearny on warships. He also had a punctured eardrum.

We were moving slowly down Main Street on the way to the police station when I spied a large sign in a bookstore window.

I jabbed Mary's arm. "Hey, look. A poster of Frank Sinatra."

"He's dreamy," she said. "Can't wait to hear him sing."

"I read a story about him in Sunday's *Daily News*. It seems the reason why Frankie isn't serving in the military is because he has a punctured eardrum."

"So?"

"So, silly girlfriend, he has the same problem as our Jimmy. Only it doesn't work for everyone. Remember our friend, Artie? He's a GI fighting in North Africa right now…and he has a punctured eardrum, too."

"Okay," she said.

Nobody cares, I thought. I didn't bother to explain how I knew, since she didn't bother to ask me, but I was there when it happened. We had gone to Coney Island for a day of fun in the sun. We were riding on the world famous *Cyclone*, the highest rollercoaster ride yet. Super high climbs, faster downs, only to sweep way up again, ready for a mightier drop. I was scared silly with my height phobia, wondering how I got talked into going. We'd just careened down another steep track when suddenly Artie's hand flew to his right ear, and he held it, his face twisted with pain. His eardrum had ruptured. Six months later, he was drafted into the Army. The ringing in his ear persisted, but they weren't about to let go of a twenty-two-year-old healthy specimen. So much for punctured eardrums keeping you out of the service.

I picked up the girls' conversation about the black seams of silk stockings.

Annie said, "I wonder if someday we can wear pants like men do? I wouldn't mind. I really don't like those stupid black seams. Oh, they're sexy when you first put them on, but they always go crooked."

Mary, who struggled to slip her jeans off her generous hips, quipped, "I wouldn't wear pants anywhere *but* here. A lady is a lady, and she doesn't wear pants when she's not working in a shipyard. Besides, as you say, the seams are sexy."

"I didn't mean work pants," Annie said. "I mean real trousers, slacks I think they're called. You know—stylish. As a matter of fact, in that magazine *Modern Screen*, Katherine Hepburn wore slacks and she looked great."

"She was just showing off. Movie stars will do anything for publicity." Mary snorted. At five-foot, and weighing in at one-hundred thirty pounds, she was voluptuous. But she was so pretty. Her green eyes flirted with the boys as she patted her dark brown, shoulder length hair, so carefully rolled under in a pageboy hairdo.

Annie, a slender five-four, was a natural blond, blue-eyed beauty. Her hair, cut in a short bob, flew about arbitrarily with the breeze and looked adorable. She was subdued, the quiet type, which worked well with the other two carpoolers, Janice and Mary, who were a bit on the wild side, full of life, searching for excitement.

And me, I was somewhere in between. A shade shorter than Annie, I was all of five-foot-two-inches. Artie was a tease. He would sing, *Five Foot Two, Eyes of Blue*, except my eyes were more green than blue. My hair, a shiny-brown-touch-of-red, was naturally wavy and hung long and free. During work, I kept it tied in a bandana-style kerchief like all the lady welders in the Yard.

"Wearing pants here is necessary," I said. "They protect our legs from burns. Although it did take some getting used to." I giggled, remembering how uncomfortable it felt at first.

"Would *you* wear these ugly things anywhere else but in the Yard?" Mary asked.

Over the neighing of negative exclamations, Annie squealed, "Heck, no. I wouldn't dare go *anywhere* dressed this way. Imagine the looks we'd get."

The car couldn't keep out the cold, and I shivered in the snowy winter weather. "Right now, I'm grateful for my heavy work pants," I said, through chattering teeth.

But I knew what Annie meant. I, too, disliked the annoying black line on silk hose, the way it always moved this way and that on the leg. In warmer weather, we girls sometimes cheated. We would draw a line down the back of our legs, dispensing with stockings altogether. It was cheaper, too. With the war on, silk was becoming scarce. These days you could buy stockings made out of nylon, a manmade material invented to replace the silk in parachutes. It was guaranteed not to run like silk hose. They were nicer, softer, and stayed up better. But they were expensive. This last Christmas, I received a pair as a gift. I saved them for special occasions.

The idea of women wearing men's trousers really hit the mark when I was getting into the car. My jeans felt good just then. If I'd been wearing a skirt, I'd have to hold it carefully while I struggled to get into the ice-cold back seat. Still, the idea *was* wild. What lady would wear trousers on a date? It would never happen, Miss Hepburn or not. But I had to agree they were more comfortable than skirts. They might even be fun to wear as long as they weren't made of that stiff denim material they used to make our work jeans. Yes, I *could* see wearing them, if they were made of flowing, colorful fabrics.

"Zelda, we're at the Police Station," Jimmy said, breaking into my reverie.

I looked out the window at a squat, red-brick building. Tall, double-glass doors swung in and out as men went off duty and others arrived. Kearny Police Station changed shifts at four-thirty each afternoon. Seeing the men in their navy blue uniforms brought home my feelings of urgency. They had to find Janice.

As I entered, the sergeant on duty glanced over at me from his desk. He sat on a raised platform in the center of the busy room. I waited while he completed a call.

That done, he beckoned to me. "Yes?"

I looked up at the officer and said, "I'd like to report a missing person."

A benign expression played across his round, flushed face. "When and where did this—" he waved his hands, "missing person occur?"

Did he think he was addressing a child, or some ninny? I ignored it.

"My friend, Janice, carpools with us. She hasn't been seen since yesterday at the Yard. She didn't show for the drive home. She didn't come in today, hasn't phoned to let us know. No one has seen her since yesterday morning. I called her home." I couldn't hold back a bite in my voice, even as I lied. I was desperate he should take me seriously.

The police sergeant leaned back in his chair, his bulky stomach reaching to the lip of his desk. His narrow eyes examined me, up and down. I felt ill-at-ease, standing there in my work pants and boots.

When he was apparently satisfied that I wasn't a prankster, he picked up the telephone. His fleshy fist encircled the phone's long neck as he jiggled the handle. With the receiver to his ear, he spoke into the mouthpiece, his voice loud. "John, I have a young lady here reporting a missing person."

The detective who came toward us reminded me of that movie actor, Robert Taylor. Wavy, blue-black hair escaped from a gray Fedora pushed to the back of his head, showing off a widows-peak hairline. His leather jacket, open and casual, hung from wide shoulders. He was the same height, too, about five-ten, a solidly built body showing strength. Then he smiled, teeth gleaming in the overhead lights. Oh, God, he was gorgeous.

"Detective John O'Reilly will help you," the Sergeant said.

I came down off my cloud and smiled, nodding stupidly.

We walked to his desk in a corner of the large room, surrounded by other desks. He pointed to a chair across from him. "Have a seat."

I sat.

"Tell me about this missing person, Miss, er?"

"Zelda Bea," I said, holding out my hand.

He hesitated, then reached over and touched it briefly like he wasn't accustomed to shaking hands with complainants in the police station. He waved me to go on.

Here goes, I thought. "I work at Kearny Federal. Yesterday, my friend, Janice, and I were assigned to the top deck of the USS Turner. I left Janice in the locker room—she was to meet me in a few minutes by the ladder taking us to the top. I haven't seen her since. No one I questioned in the yard admits to seeing her since our arrival that day. Joe Morgan, our foreman, said he sent her on an errand. When I asked again later, he acted impatient and waved me off. Then she left a note saying she went somewhere with someone. I don't think she would have done that without telling me. We were to work together."

He nodded but said nothing.

I glared at the detective as my angst built, my eyes never wavering. "More to the point, she carpools with me and two other girls and our driver. It is normal to travel to and from work together. She didn't go home with us last night. She didn't come in this morning. We haven't seen her all day."

I waited as he wrote something in his pad.

"Did I tell you she has a three-year-old son, Billy, and her mother, Sadie, living with her? She's a very responsible mother. She would *never* just up and leave them without a word."

Why hadn't I thought of that before? She must have left word with them. I had to call Sadie as soon as I got home. I needed to find out if she had heard from Janice.

"Detective, she would tell me if she was leaving work without us. Unless she couldn't." I made eye contact, hoping how I felt would show. "We always call our driver if we won't be there. She hasn't. Something about this whole thing scares the beejeebees out of me."

He wrote some more in his pad, not even looking at me.

Did he think I was being hysterical over nothing?

I tried to put some steel into my voice. "Janice *is* missing, Detective."

"Has anyone else questioned your friend's disappearance?" He leaned forward in his chair while tipping his hat farther back with a forefinger, his expression somber.

Gosh, I'd seen Taylor do it just that way in *The Detective*.

"Miss Bea, you haven't answered me. Has anyone else questioned her disappearance?"

I felt my face grow hot. "Well, yes, our driver and the girls who ride with us."

O'Reilly wrote while I spoke. He looked up, rubbing his chin. "And no one saw Miss Bates after arriving at the Yard yesterday?"

My fingers gripped the chair. "I didn't mention her last name. Has someone else reported her missing?"

"Please answer the question."

Slowly, I shook my head. "I asked around. No one on the deck had seen her. And no one on the ground, either."

"So you told Mr. Morgan and Mr. Hansen."

"How did you know I spoke to Mr. Hansen?"

Instead of answering, he indicated the paper he'd written on. "Would you be willing to sign what you said here after I have it typed?"

"You *will* be investigating, Detective?" I stared at him. "We haven't seen her since yesterday morning." I clenched my jaw. I had to stop repeating myself, stop wringing my hands. I'd done all I could. "I'll sign it."

He stood. "I won't be long."

Five minutes later, O'Reilly returned and handed me a typewritten copy. After a quick perusal, I said, "Where do I put my name?"

I signed, and that was it. I left. The Sergeant at the front desk smiled when I passed him. Maybe he was being nice. Or maybe not. Do they hear so much of missing persons they become immune to it? I hoped that wasn't the case.

I had been in police headquarters twenty minutes.

Jimmy glanced up when I opened the door. "How'd it go?"

"Okay, I guess. Detective O'Reilly promised to look into it. We'll just have to wait and see." I inhaled deeply, grateful to smell fresh, cold air, to flush away the stale stink of the cigarette smoke permeating the stationhouse.

I was quiet as we started the ride home. Melancholy songs wafted from the radio, soft and sweet. Sad music for a sad time. The Andrews Sisters sang *Don't sit under the apple tree with anyone else but me, 'til I come marching home.*

Sure, they were singing to all the GIs away from home in some foreign land or out to sea, but I felt they were referring to Janice, too. She was supposed to be working on war ships. Only she never showed up. Why hadn't she called? Why hadn't she let us know where she was? Why wasn't she sitting there now, riding home with us? We should be kidding around, laughing at some silly joke, deciding which restaurant we would stop at tomorrow night.

Instead, I felt scared deep down in my bones. Something terrible had happened. And I seemed to be the only one concerned.

CHAPTER SEVEN

Jimmy's radio played non-stop as we made our way home. I heard the lyrics *I'll get by as long as I have you...* I thought of all my friends drafted into the service. The world had become a scary place to live. War was frightening.

I leaned into the recess of the seat and closed my eyes. When I heard the words *we'll meet again, don't know where, don't know when...* it carried me back to when we were still young. Was it only a year or two ago? We were silly and innocent and happy, our small group of good friends. We thought we were so grown up. Nothing could interfere with our plans. We had things to do. Places to see. That was before the insanity of war changed all our lives.

I remembered how we used to pile into that little black Ford with the rumble seat. There'd been a funny joke going around. *Ford can be purchased in any color as long as it is black*. I chuckled.

Annie turned and looked at me.

"I was thinking about the song they just played," I told her. "Remember all the good times we had? Artie was the only one old enough to own a car. Now, guys his age are old enough to be drafted, and girls work on ships."

Annie looked pensive. "Do you think we *will* all meet again someday?"

"I hope so. I liked those times before the war when we walked to Clinton Hall to dance. Sometimes even a big band played there. I'll never forget one time before the war. Gene Krupa came to entertain us. I can see him now, beating wildly at his drums, sweat running off his brow, hair flying, and a wide grin on his handsome face. I stood by the bandstand watching his every move—sticks flying, drums booming. Remember his songs?"

"I remember *Sing, Sing, Sing. Drum Boogie*, and... and... remember *High on a Windy Hill?*"

"We danced the Jitterbug to all of them," I said.

A smile lingered on her pretty face. "What about all the times we hitched rides to the picture show or the ice cream shop in that cute Ford of Artie's? Think we'll ever do that again?"

"Poor Artie drove us everywhere. Remember the time when one of the boys suggested we go to Long Island to see the Decoration Day parade? Everyone else wanted to go on a picnic. Except Artie, and he had the car. I wanted to be a part of the celebration, too, so I went with them. I'd never traveled that far on the island, and the day was perfect for it. The sun was bright, the air clear."

"I remember," she said with a faraway look. "Wish I'd gone."

I left Annie to her own thoughts as I drifted into that particular memory. It was spring. We rode the Southern State Parkway east through Nassau into Suffolk County. I saw farms sprouting new growth, trees wearing pretty fresh greenery. The countryside dazzled with the scent of early flowers flaunting every color in the rainbow.

Just past Riverhead, we took the south fork. From Montauk Highway, we made a right onto Mill Road. The little town of Westhampton Beach sat parallel to the Atlantic shoreline. Eventually, we turned onto Main Street.

Automobiles lined both sides of the very wide, very crowded avenue, but we found parking on a side street. Red, white and blue banners hung in the front windows of the tiny shops crowded with displays of beach gear, antiques, ethnic foods... And people, so many people filled the streets.

We were early for the parade. We strolled down to the beach, kicked off our shoes and ran on the hard, wet sand. I felt the heat on my face, on my arms. The guys rolled their pant legs to their knees. They threw handfuls of water my way. I screamed. I laughed.

"Wish I had my trunks," Artie said. "I swam in water colder than this."

The salt water lapped at my feet. I felt like a little kid, and I giggled. "Not for me. I'll wait for summer."

Just then, the blaring of bugles and the rolling of drums announced the grand festivities had started.

"Let's go," the boys yelled. They staggered behind me as they rearranged their pant cuffs.

As we hurried back to Main Street, I heard taps played on a trumpet, and then three loud cannon shots. We were in time to catch the American Flag being raised. I saw it going up a long pole, slowly lowered to half-mast. It flapped in a slight breeze. Men and women lined the curb, hands over their hearts, reciting the Pledge of Allegiance. Young children sat on their father's shoulders, happy grins on their faces as they vigorously waved small flags. We clapped, whistled, and cheered along with them.

The band marched by, trailed by the town dignitaries waving from a long, open car. Bringing up the rear were the World War I veterans, wearing uniforms, medals, and somber faces. Some walked, some limped, and some rode in wheel chairs, keeping pace with the beat of the drums. I watched bystanders dab handkerchiefs at their eyes. I dabbed, too. How could I not?

When the parade had passed, the three of us looked at each other, smiled, and crossed the street to the ice cream parlor. All that activity was hungry work. Gals and guys filled most of the small round tables. We found an empty one and feasted on hotdogs with mustard and sauerkraut and a shared Coca Cola.

Though it was still spring, the wind blew soft and warm. People dressed in summer clothing. It was a great day to be an American on a holiday commemorating our war heroes. And it was vacation time. The east end of Long Island, known as *The Hamptons,* was rated as having *the* best beaches in the U.S. of A. It was a great place to stage a memorial to our service men.

It was a small event, as such things go. It was nothing near the elaborate Fifth Avenue parade that went on and on for blocks. But I was happy to be there, to share the honor with our heroes. I hoped to never forget those veterans I saw that day, the proud men who fought bravely in a war promising to end all wars.

I heard Annie and Mary chatting away as I looked up from my daydream, the images still fresh. I couldn't help but think here we were again, in the middle of world war number two, our brave men fighting across the same seas, and for the same stupid reasons. How many more would die or come home in wheelchairs, battered and broken and bruised, before they learned a better way to stop tyrants? We invented so many great things to make our lives easier, but we never learned how to live in a world without war.

Zelda the Welder

My throat choked up, and I wanted to cry. I stared out the car window instead, passing the time reading war posters.

Support the Troops, Buy War Bonds, caught my eye. Every week when I received my paycheck, I bought a war bond. It made me feel I was doing something special for our boys overseas. That's what it was all about, wasn't it, helping our country? Was there more I could do, I wondered?

I watched the billboards go by. The posters continued the length of the highway. So many messages.

Mary called suddenly, "Hey, take a gander at that."

I looked where she pointed. The poster touted *Buy Defense Bonds and Stamps*. A pilot in uniform was smiling, planes flying the skies around him, his thumb gesturing up. The sign read, *You buy 'em, we'll fly 'em!* He sure was handsome.

"I'd buy a hundred bonds if he came with them," Mary said, giggling.

Annie smiled. "Gosh, he looks swell." She turned around in the front seat to look at Mary. "I wonder if he has a brother. You know, one for you and one for me. Maybe another for Zelda."

"Girls, some respect, please," Jimmy said. In his rearview mirror, I saw his lips twitch in a smile.

Then Mary let out a squeal and pointed to a billboard we were approaching. This poster was of a sailor. He was walking away, his face turned back toward us, his white hat sitting jauntily over one eyebrow. He wore a serious expression. The caption, on a blood-red background read *If you tell where he's going... he may never get there!*

My stomach quaked, and I brought my hand to my mouth. It was what he had draped over his shoulder, a rope tied to a large, bulging duffle bag. The bag was bent in such a way there could be anything inside. It looked so much like the bag I saw on the deck of the DE it might have been its twin. But of course that was crazy. I knew that. My eyes were playing tricks. Still...

"Jimmy. Slow down. Please," I said, as we got closer. "That poster. See the bag he's carrying? That's what I saw on board the DE. Just that way."

"You saw *that* bag?" Mary said.

"No. Of course not *that* bag. But it looked exactly the same, bulges and all. And the color—"

"Now, honey," Annie chimed in, "don't get excited. Maybe you did see a similar bag. So what? That doesn't prove Janice has been whisked away in one. That *is* what you're really thinking, isn't it?"

I slumped in my seat. What was the use? They didn't understand. No one did. And Annie was right. It *was* just a duffle bag stuffed with normal gear.

I listened to the music and glanced out the window at the evening traffic. The girls dozed. I couldn't sleep. I was too wound up. My best friend could be hurt or in serious trouble. Then again, she could be someplace having fun while I sat worried and miserable.

Perhaps I *was* getting too worked up. Perhaps the girls were right. I hoped so. I would have good reason to give Janice hell for not letting me know where she went. I could rest easy with that.

We left New Jersey into New York. In Manhattan, we took the Midtown Tunnel into Queens. I felt I was in a void in the two-lane passageway under the East River, cars speeding ahead and behind.

The girls woke as we reached the Long Island side. Love songs wafted around us, and we sang along with the melancholy music. Intended to be comforting to those waiting behind, they were instead sad songs, like *It's Only a Paper Moon, shining over a make believe sky,* and *Ain't Misbehavin', just sav'n my love for you.* The words ate at my heartstrings. The song *Don't Get Around Much Anymore, might have gone, but what for...* spoke my feelings out loud, and I did cry silent tears.

  I thought of all the women working in the Yard whose young husbands or sons or brothers were fighting over there right at that moment. When they returned… If they returned… Perhaps, one day we would greet *our* returning heroes, like the men I saw in the parade. Maybe this war *would be* the last war.

  My favorite song came on, the lyrics resonating as the music played, and I hummed along. *Blue Moon, I am no longer alone, without a love in my life, without a love of my own...* No longer alone. That's what it was all about, wasn't it?

CHAPTER EIGHT

When Jimmy's car pulled up to my house, I hadn't even noticed we were on my street. I opened my door and jumped out, waving goodbye to Jimmy and the girls. As I ran inside, my missing friend played on my mind. I intended to see Janice's mother, Sadie, right away. Perhaps she could tell me where Janice went. She *should* have heard from her daughter by now.

I expected Meow to be happy to see me and eager for his dinner. He would sidle up and rub my ankle. Not so tonight. When I walked in the front door, he jumped from his sentinel perch on the windowsill, stared at me in that superior way of his, then ran to my bedroom to hide under the bed. That told me he had been worried and was, therefore, very angry with me. It was seven-thirty. I wasn't usually *this* late getting home without leaving extra goodies for his evening meal. Gone all day while he waited for his dinner. It was unforgivable.

I took some leftover tuna salad from the icebox and placed a spoonful into his dish. I whispered softly as I tried to coax him out from his hiding place. He would have none of it.

"Some really nice nibbles are waiting for you," I said sweetly. He was being a brat of a cat. "Okay, be like that. It's your loss. I have more important things to think about."

Janice's little boy, Billy, came to mind. He was the cutest three-year-old. And he was smart, too, in that sweet, innocent way of children. I loved the little fellow. He was in his Grandma Sadie's keep when his mom was at work. Even as I hoped Janice might be home with him now, I knew it wasn't so.

I changed my clothes. While I hastened to put my lunch things away, my stomach reminded me I'd had only a light lunch a long time ago. The rest of the tuna salad would stop my rumbling stomach. I also ate one of the cookies Ida had given me. Then I wrapped one for Billy and two for Sadie.

Before I set off, I stopped at Ida's to give her a cup of sugar. I would have liked

Zelda the Welder

to stay and comfort her, to ease that lost look in her eyes, but it was already eight o'clock. I got *in my merry Oldsmobile,* as the song went, and headed to Janice's place. I hoped for answers from Sadie—or suggestions on where to get some.

With gas rationing, I used my car sparingly. I had half a tank left. It had to last to the end of the month, two weeks away. I drove to Janice's building, parked, then walked the three flights to apartment 3D.

At the Bates' door, I knocked. Minutes passed. *I should have called, told her I was coming.* Just as I started to walk away, I heard the latch release. The door opened slowly.

Sadie peeked out. She stood there, all of four-foot-ten-inches tall, in her pretty blue housedress, starchy and sweet smelling, and her crop of tight white curls.

When she saw me, her broad grin brightened the doorway. "Why hello, Zelda. How nice to see you."

I smiled back. "Hello, Sadie." I bent to address Janice's sweet three-year-old son who was clinging to his grandmother's leg, one chubby cheek pressed against the cotton fabric of her dress. Taking in his curly red hair, his large blue eyes so much like his mom's, I felt a pang of concern. "Hi, Billy."

He looked so innocent staring up at me. Sadie tapped gently on Billy's head. Thumb in his mouth, he managed a soft, "Hi."

Time to ask the question. But how to word it? Should I just say, *Hey, guess what, your daughter's gone missing. And she could be dead to boot. What do you know about it*? No, I couldn't hurt this woman when I wasn't sure about anything. I crossed my fingers behind me. I'd settled for half a lie. "Sadie, I'm sorry to disturb you so late. Is Janice here? I didn't talk to her today."

Sadie shook her head. "She's not home yet. We didn't see her this morning. She leaves so early, we usually miss her. Last night, we were asleep before she came home. Sometimes, she doesn't come home for dinner. She tries to call, but it doesn't always get through. The party line—" All of a sudden, her brow creased. "You didn't see her today? Didn't you drive in together?"

My face grew hot. "Well…"

"Oh, where are my manners? Come in. Come in." She led me into her tidy living room and motioned to the couch. "Please.

Sit. I'll bring us some nice tea. I won't be but a minute."

I sat, trying to relax. Janice's apartment had the coziness of Colonial American style furniture. Stained wood shutters added to the nostalgia of the country's earlier days. Next to the brick fireplace stood an antique spinning wheel. I had been with her and Billy on the long drive to Long Island's east end when she'd spotted it at that shop in Southampton. Janice loved her home. I knew she also loved her son and her mother. So why hadn't she gotten in touch with them, if only to say where she was and when she'd be back?

I was glad I stopped in to speak to Sadie. It was kinder than talking on a cold telephone. Now, I knew she hadn't seen Janice either. Now, I was sure the whole business wasn't my fanciful imagination.

Just then, Sadie carried in the tea. I reached into my purse for Ida's cookies. As I unwrapped the package, Billy's eyes lit up. He glanced at his grandmother.

She nodded, and he carefully took one in his tiny hand. I wanted to hug him, but he was so shy, I just gave him a warm smile. He actually smiled back.

Janice, you have a sweet kid. He wants his mom. Where are you?

As I sipped my tea, my mind whirled with questions. I needed answers.

"Sadie, did Janice ever mention a boyfriend?"

"She goes to dinner once in a while, but she comes home alone."

"Would you know of anyone whom she could be out with now?"

"Why are you asking these questions? Wouldn't she tell *you* if she had a fella'. You're her best friend. I'm only her mother." She smiled.

That was her try at flippancy. I tried to smile back, but I couldn't handle funny. "Does she know anyone in Miami?"

"Zelda, you're frightening me." Her face became somber, her eyes questioning. "Where is my daughter?"

"Sadie, she drove to work with us yesterday. I left her at the locker room—" I stopped. I hadn't wanted to tell her that much. I cleared my throat.

Sadie leaned toward me. "Do you remember when Janice wanted to join the WASP for the flight training program? Of course, she couldn't. She had Billy to think of. But she talks about it sometimes. She wouldn't do that without telling us, would she?"

"I wouldn't think so, but you know your headstrong daughter. I wouldn't worry, Sadie. She'll call as soon as she finds the time."

Billy stood by Sadie's chair nibbling his cookie, his chin resting on one chubby palm as he leaned on his grandmother's lap. He glanced up, eyes at half-mast, a cookie-crumb grin on his sleepy face.

Time to make a hasty retreat before I say anything more.

I put down my cup and stood. "It's late. I won't keep you and Billy up any longer. Thanks for the tea." I took her small hand in mine. "And Sadie, if you need anything before Janice gets back, please call me. Day or night."

Sadie's eyes fixed on mine. "Now I am worried. Please, will you find out where she is?"

"You bet. And I'll let you know, if she doesn't first." I smiled. That was the best I could do.

Walking back down the stairs, I questioned what I had learned from Sadie.

Okay, Janice occasionally went out to dinner. We girls went out together once in a while, mostly on Fridays. Was that what she referred to, or was there something more Janice hadn't bothered to mention to me?

I reached my car. The door handle was frozen, and I had to pound with my shoe to break the thin layer of ice and open it. The seat felt like a block of ice. Even with gloves on, my fingers ached as they gripped the steering wheel. It would be nice if cars had small radiators, like houses do. Wild thought. Why would anyone think of putting heat in cars?

Anxious to get home, I raced along doing thirty-five. I spotted a distinctive white, green, and black police car ahead and slowed. I didn't need a speeding ticket to end this memorable day. Every second tore at my nerves until I parked before my house. A welcoming light glowed in the window. I rushed to open the door. Inside smelled cozy and warm. The coal furnace was working well. My tension eased.

I took a steaming-hot bath, then slipped on pajamas and a warm robe. I brushed my teeth, combed my hair, smeared a glob of Ponds cream on my face, and went to the kitchen. From the icebox, I took out the bottle of milk. I poured some into a small pot, heating it slowly over the gas flame. Five minutes took the chill off. Some went into Meow's dish, now empty of tuna. The rest went into my cup. We both should sleep well tonight.

Grumbling softly, sweet Meow left his hiding place to partake of the delicacy. As he lapped up the milk, he kept his back to me. He hadn't forgiven me for deserting him, although he readily took my gift of apology.

I removed the drip pan from under the icebox, emptied it, and then replaced it. Nightly chores completed, save one. I hadn't put Janice out of my mind. If I wanted to sleep, I needed to do that. Seated at the kitchen table, I removed the cover from my portable Royal typewriter. Hands poised above the keys, I paused. Okay, Janice had disappeared. Much had transpired since. Perhaps if I saw everything in print, something would spring out and make sense.

Janice, help me find you, I typed. *Tell me where you are. I'm listening.*

I stared at the keyboard, picturing her as I'd seen her yesterday morning—

smiling and happy, and eager to work on the top deck.

Meow settled on the table, his tail swishing the air slowly, head resting on his front paws. With one eye open, one eye closed, he watched me type.

Questions flowed from my fingertips. What did I really know?

There was Big Joe's story that he sent Janice on an errand—and his refusal to explain what that errand was. He avoided my questions as easily as he avoided my eyes. Oh, he was slick all right.

When Janice left the locker room, did she board the ship without me? No one admitted to seeing her. Not on the DE, and not on the ground.

Did she have dinner with someone, as Sadie suggested? Perhaps. But how could that have anything to do with her going missing from the top deck of an unfinished destroyer escort?

Unfinished DE? *The shed.* My hand flew to my mouth. It struck me—the wastepaper basket, the cut-up newspaper. Only Big Joe and I had seen the note that had been in my vest pocket. Except the person who put it there.

Check the shed first thing in the morning. See if the newspaper is still there.

But what should I do if the cut up words fit? What if that really was blood on the floor? And what if I knew the person or persons on the DE who was responsible?

With a sigh, I typed the final question still plaguing me.

Why Janice—?

I looked up when the clock chimed eleven. My vision blurred with fatigue. I slipped the cover back on my typewriter. Meow closed both eyes and opened his mouth in a wide, luxurious yawn.

Time to turn off my thoughts and the lights. Tomorrow I would visit the shed. I placed the typewritten page on top of the newspaper note and put both in a kitchen drawer.

CHAPTER NINE

Tired as I was, I was sure I would not be able to sleep a wink. And then the alarm pealed. Five a.m. Time to get up and face the new day. I groaned, rolled over, and pulled the covers to my chin. Meow purred loudly as he plopped atop me, whiskers tickling my nose.

"I know. I know," I said. "It's breakfast time."

I dressed, ate, and put together a lunch. In a small suitcase, I packed a change of clothes for the evening. The girls and I always packed a change of clothes on Fridays. We brought along skirts—nine inches from the floor does it—and colorful sweaters. In our heavy woolen coats and jaunty little hats, we turned from rough-and-ready shipyard workers to nice young ladies ready for a pleasant night out.

Sometimes, we stopped for dinner or a movie. If the time were right, we would stop at Clinton Hall for a dance or two with the lonely soldiers. We were never too tired for that.

Today was special. It was Mary's birthday. The four of us had planned to cut out of work early and see Frank Sinatra at the Paramount. Only I wasn't in much of a party mood. Maybe I would bow out. Annie could go with her.

As I walked outside, for a split second I thought I saw Janice in the car. But she wasn't there. Annie wasn't there either.

I climbed into the back. "Where's Annie?"

"She can't make it today," Jimmy said. "Her mother's sick."

"Oh," I said. "I'm sorry to hear that."

"Looks like it's just you and me, girlfriend," Mary said from the front seat. "Jimmy, remember that we won't be going home with you tonight. We're hitching a ride to New York City."

Jimmy nodded. "You girls be careful, now."

"Yes, mother." Mary turned and gave me a dazzling smile.

I smiled back, resolved to have a good time. I wouldn't spoil Mary's birthday for the world.

When we arrived at Kearny, I got some welcomed news. Big Joe wanted me up on the DE again. He wanted me to finish the work that had been disrupted by the snow yesterday. That would give me a chance to check the wastepaper basket in the shed. I filled my bucket with rods. Adjusting my gear, I approached the ladder that would take me to the top deck. I reached out, ready to start the trip up.

Suddenly, something crashed to the ground beside me. For a moment, my hand grasped at nothing. I grabbed for a rung, my hand shaking, heart pounding. Inches away, a four-foot metal spear stuck up from the cement walk. I stumbled back, trembling so bad I dropped my bucket. Welding rods spread on the walk like a game of pick-up sticks.

The steel had pierced the cement, cracking it in a zigzag pattern. Four-inches thick and four-feet long, it leaned at a slight tilt just short of the ladder—and me.

Eyes wide, I gazed up the length of the ladder. I saw no one. Had the piece of scrap fallen on purpose? Was it a message meant to frighten me, to keep me quiet about Janice being missing? No, of course not. I was being melodramatic, irrational. It was just an accident. Of course, it was.

Workers came running toward me. Someone called out, "Are you all right?"

Before I could answer, Big Joe came from somewhere in the yard and put his arm around my shoulder, guiding me away from the fallen metal.

"You okay?" he asked.

"Fine," I said, my voice sounding off-key and shaky. I tried to laugh it off, but my raw nerves had me shivering.

"Some waste metal must have rolled off the deck. It shouldn't have been left lying around. The wind. You could have been killed." He looked up to where it had come from. "Want to sit it out for a while?"

"I can work."

"You sure?"

"Not a problem," I said, my stomach rolling inside me all the while.

Big Joe stared at me. Then he walked to the steel spear. He pulled and yanked and pulled again. Finally, he was able to wrench out the rod. With an angry glint in his eyes, the metal still in his hand, he climbed the ladder and disappeared over the top of the towering ship.

How easily he climbs, I thought. Now, it was my turn. I took hold of the thin electric line, uncurled it, and set out to drag it up the ladder behind me. It was easier today. My mind was on things other than being afraid of the height. I would finish my section of the top deck and never, ever climb that high again, job or no job. I wouldn't allow myself to think any farther ahead at the moment. But I had to get up there.

With any luck, they hadn't emptied the wastebasket.

On deck, I placed my rod and bucket at the section I was to finish. The shed was about twenty-five feet away. Casually, I sauntered to it.

The door was locked. A nasty word salted my tongue as I took my hand from the doorknob. Some men who were working on another project stood close by, but I had no feasible excuse to have one of them open the storeroom for me. Besides, I didn't know whom Janice had met up with. I had to be careful.

I set about my work, trying to concentrate on welding, but that, too, failed me. My line wouldn't spark properly. It wouldn't melt the metal. I tried several times. Instead of the rod sparking and the plate's metal absorbing it, the spark flubbed out. The tip flared too brightly, then fizzled. Instead of a nice even weld creating a bead as it joined the two plates, the melted steel made a gully, ruining the neat edge of the plate. It caused ugly clumps. Where was my beautiful, even bead?

I thought of asking one of the men for help, but decided against it. The only thing to do was to go down and get another line.

I left everything as it lay and walked to the ladder. Only the ladder wasn't there. Just the wide-open expanse of courtyard. Mary stood below, warming herself by a coal stove. I waved and called down to her.

Suddenly, I felt hands on my shoulders. Someone pulled me backwards.

"Hey, hey, be careful. You don't want to stand that close to the edge. It's a long way down."

It was Big Joe. With his usual grin.

I pointed. "How do I get down, Joe? And maybe you know what happened to the electric? First my line is too hot, then it turns cold. The plate's a mess." I was seething, trying hard not to let the tears lining my lashes roll down my cheeks. Someone was playing tricks on me. Why?

I had to admit, Big Joe looked puzzled. Either he was one hell of an actor or he really didn't know what was going on. I gave him the benefit of the doubt.

"Now what, Joe?"

He gave the missing ladder a dismissive glance. "Follow me." He turned and began walking to the far side of the deck. "I guess they didn't know you were up here."

"And my line? They didn't see my line going up the ladder? They just shut it off?"

Although he smiled, his voice was anything but merry. "You know, kid, you worry too much. Need anything, just call me. You know I can give you anything you need." He raised an eyebrow and let his eyes explore me. His expression looked, well, slimy was the best word I could think of. "This ladder is always in place." He pointed. "It's the one the painters use."

"Thanks," I bit out. Smartass. He was getting smarmy on me and it made me nervous. How does one make the boss behave? Especially when one is three decks above the ground?

"Joe, I'd rather work below. The height makes me dizzy."

He studied me with that penetrating look I'd come to recognize. When he answered, his tone rang of dismissal. "Okay. Go on down. But you'll need a new line, wherever you work." He moved away.

I looked around the vast upper deck, to the shed, and then to the skinny ladder. "This whole place makes me sick," I grumbled under my breath, "and to hell with the newspapers in the shed."

Big Joe turned his head like he'd heard. Too bad, I shrugged. Clinging to the ladder and holding my breath, I descended.

Mary waited for me by the fire as I came around the edge of the ship. Nothing blocked the wind here. The air got colder by the second. The sun hid behind dark clouds, refusing to come out and warm us. The sky looked like a snowstorm in the making.

Mary's eyes danced with excitement. "Zelda, look at this weather. We can't do any good here. How about we take off now?"

I looked up. Flurries stung my face like ice pellets. It *would* be impossible to work.

Mary stared at me, her head tilted. "You all right? You don't look so good. Something happen up there?"

Better not tell her my feelings right then about Federal, the metal spear, the dumb ladder, and Mister Big wearing that sloppy grin while he undressed me with his eyes. "I'm fine," I said.

The wind gusted, and I pulled my scarf close. The weather was turning nasty. Snowflakes swirled in great globs. I could barely see the ships as they rolled and bounced in their slips. If a blizzard was coming our way, it would be impossible to work outside.

"Yeah. Let's get out of here before the weather gets any worse."

Mary smiled happily.

In the locker room, I slipped on my red plaid skirt and white turtleneck sweater. I pulled my red wool hat over my ears, jaunty-like, and swept my red scarf over the shoulder of my coat. Then we hooked a ride to New York.

CHAPTER TEN

Adrenaline pumped in my veins as the Chevy slowed and pulled to the side to let us out. We were in New York City. Theatre marques blinked up and down the Avenue. *The Maltese Falcon. One Million BC. Pinocchio*. Even in broad daylight, they glared and sparkled. I loved the movies, and Times Square, and everything about New York. This was the place to be.

"Thanks for the lift, Sammy," I said as I stepped from the backseat.

Sammy, an older gentleman, had driven us in from Kearny. We were lucky he'd been going our way.

Mary followed me out of the car, waving as he honked his horn and pulled away.

Adjusting my scarf, I glanced around at the teeming crowd. Forty Second Street moved. Times Square swarmed. That was one of the things that fascinated me most about this busy, wonderful city. No matter what time of day, what time of night, what season or the weather, people filled the sidewalks, five and six across, sometimes spilling over into the road.

The snowstorm in Jersey hadn't reached New York, and hopefully it wouldn't. The sun shone brightly in the sapphire sky. Not a cloud to break the mood. I stood beside Mary feeling a huge grin stretch my lips.

Maybe it had been a good thing that we'd cut out when we did. I was no nearer to finding Janice, and Big Joe was fast becoming a hindrance. I needed the break.

"What now?" I asked Mary.

"Now we enjoy the show." Taking my gloved hand, she pulled me along with the herd.

Whether you were on foot or in a vehicle, it was the traffic lights that set the tempo. STOP. WAIT. Move on *en masse* to the next short block. Traveling uptown, downtown, cross-town. Continuous. Purposeful. This was *my* city.

The line waiting for tickets outside the *Paramount Theatre* at 1501 Broadway continued around the block. Bobbysoxers were everywhere. Kids stood three and four abreast at some points, and they kept coming even as we moved forward. The young girls were bundled in wool coats riding just above the pleated, below-the-knee skirts. Knit scarves in red or green were wrapped around and around their necks, and matching wool hats were pulled low over their ears.

I could see they had come in groups. I bet many high school students cut out early this Friday. That wouldn't be a problem. The *Paramount Theatre* held four thousand seats. The girls shouted and elbowed one another. Their ages were between fourteen and sixteen, maybe a few seventeen-year-olds. It was hard to believe they were only a few years younger than me. Somehow, once you hit twenty you had to be grown-up. I would never scream over an entertainer. Never. How gross. Babies.

Also in the mix waiting to get tickets were older ladies, some in their twenties and early thirties. They dressed more formally, skirts and jackets and brimmed hats. Likely, they had just come from the office.

We waited in line for the theatre to open, but we didn't need to wait for tickets. Mary had purchased four of them weeks in advance. She sold the extra pair of tickets to two ladies waiting in line, and all was well. The doors opened, and the crowd stampeded forward. Once Mary and I were in the packed lobby, ushers directed us up a wide staircase. We took our seats in the balcony. I saw the whole audience from that vantage point. Even before the music started, the seats were filled to capacity. Girls stood in the back of the theatre and in the aisles.

The lights dimmed, the stage lit, and Benny Goodman's theme song, *Let's Dance,* began playing softly. The *King of Swing,* baton in hand, made the introduction.

Then Frank Sinatra walked on stage, and some four thousand voices filled the air for this cute, skinny, grinning young guy. He was as thin as the microphone stand he held onto. The audience was thunderous in their delirium, and he hadn't uttered a note yet.

Mary grinned at me. I had one fleeting thought as I looked at sweet and sexy Mary bouncing in her seat like the kids— Janice and Annie were supposed to be with us today. It was a celebration, damn it.

The deafening, jubilant noise made it easy to get in the mood. All those teenagers, stomping and yelling and screaming his name. *Frank, Frank, Frank.*

Zelda the Welder

Benny Goodman stopped leading his band and stared at the crowd with a startled expression. He was standing next to the microphone when he said, "What the hell is all that?"

I heard him over the bedlam. It was obvious to me that even he had never before witnessed such adoration.

The audience was so loud, I held my hands over my ears, but I couldn't stop beaming. I loved the excitement.

I looked down at the bobbysoxers. Some of the girls looked like they'd swooned in the excitement. I nudged Mary, but her attention was on Sinatra. If I hit her on the head, she would pay me no mind. It was a never-to-be-forgotten scene. What an afternoon.

After the show, the screaming went on, carrying everyone in its wake as we pushed through the corridor and out the side door. And there we were, Mary and I, facing the maddening throng.

Frankie arrived, stopping just outside the stage entrance of the theatre. With his Fedora tilted to one side, *The Man* grinned broadly. Apparently, he intended to autograph every sort of matter handed to him.

There were so many kids, all jostling one another, waving cards and papers and programs and whatever. They spilled over into Times Square's snarling traffic. This was a moment to remember always.

Mary and I didn't wait for Sinatra's signature. We'd had it by then—what with our early morning ride to Jersey, working half the day in the cold, and then waiting outside in the cold again. Put that together with our adrenaline rising sky high in the excitement of seeing Sinatra and the Benny Goodman band. We were exhausted and hungry.

We walked the Avenue, glancing at a variety of wares in the many small shops we passed. We stopped at the *Horn and Hardart Automat* on Sixth, my favorite place for food in all New York. I loved looking through the banks and banks of tiny windows to select what to eat. I loved putting in the required nickels, hearing them fall, then lifting the window to take out the selected food—sandwiches or soups, casseroles or pastries. They had everything, and everything was beyond delicious. How did they do it?

Mary and I found an empty table and sat on ice-cream-parlor-style chairs. We ate macaroni and cheese and people-watched. One man, with just a cup of coffee in front of him, read his newspaper as casually as sitting in his own kitchen. A little kid tugged at his mother's coat as he pointed and yelled for the food he wanted. And momma, scolding him to stop the racket, bought him what he wanted.

New York, the city that never shuts down.

The scene flooded my mind with memories. "Did I ever tell you about the first time I came here?" I asked Mary. "It was before the war. One Sunday, the gang and I came to New York to see *Gone With the Wind* at the *Roxy Theatre*. After the show, we were hungry, and I was too bashful to suggest going into one of the many wonderful restaurants. Can you believe it? Me? Shy? Refusing food? But my hungry friends required sustenance. So we stopped here at the Automat. Golly, that was living."

After Mary and I finished our dinners, I purchased a huge slice of strawberry shortcake and sang *Happy Birthday to Mary.* We shared the lovely dessert. It struck me again that Annie and Janice were supposed to be with us. A sobering thought, but I was determined not to think about that tonight, and I brushed it away.

We strolled around outside for a while. The Avenue was as crowded by night as it had been by day. Store windows were bright with lights, and auras encircled the streetlamps. I wished I could stay longer in this exciting city where troubles seemed to disappear just by being there. But it was getting quite late. Time to head for home.

Mary and I walked to the subway station and down the long flight of steps leading to the various trains. Then we had to part. We had different destinations—I to Maspeth and Mary to Elmhurst. We lived close to each other by automobile, farther by subway.

I tried to be cheery when I waved so long. I had never traveled alone on a train at night, and especially didn't like standing by myself on the dimly lit, eerie, tunnel-like white concrete station platform. The space around me echoed. When my train rattled to a stop, I literally ran to the first car. It was near-empty. One lone traveler was asleep in a corner seat. I sat nervously.

At my stop, I ran up the dimly lit stairs to the street, hoping I wouldn't have to wait long for the next bus to Maspeth. It felt good to be outside, although it was biting cold and lonely as hell. The joy of breathing fresh, clean air again lasted about two minutes before icicles began to form around my nostrils. Holding my gloved hands over my nose helped. I wondered how Mary was faring on her trip home. I was glad I'd gone to New York. The trip had done more than cheer her. It had cleared my own mind. Now, perhaps I *could* find some answers to the dilemma that was Janice.

The fifteen minutes I waited for my bus felt more like fifty. Buildings cast dark shadows that seemed to take on a persona of their own. Trees became the silhouettes of people, ever moving, ever closer.

Utter foolishness, I admonished myself, stomping the ground to circulate warmth and chase the goblins. I huddled deeper into my coat to shut out the cold, which was becoming more penetrating by the second.

Shadows seemed to grow closer, and time to move slower. At one point, I thought I saw a car like Big Joe's big black Lincoln inch by ever so slowly. A lone man drove it. I thought I saw his head turn. Was he looking at me as he passed? I shrank into my coat as if it could shield me from him.

How stupid. You must stop this.

At last, I saw the bus moving my way. It stopped in front of me. I ran up the two steps, put change in the slot, and smiled at the driver. I nodded to the men and women already aboard. Humans. I found an empty seat by a window. That felt better.

A few blocks later, a nice-looking man boarded and sat in the empty seat next to me. He smiled. "Good evening."

I returned the smile then turned away to stare at the darkness outside, hoping he wouldn't try to start a conversation.

At my stop I got off, relieved when the man sitting next to me didn't follow. I *was* getting paranoid. Still, I walked quickly along the quiet streets. It was close to midnight, and I had three long, silent blocks to walk. I tried whistling softly, but gave it up when my lips grew stiff, and the sharp air smarted my nose and brought tears to my eyes.

The half moon cast shadows under leafless maple trees lining the curb, and I hurried from shadow to shadow. Most of the houses were dark, but for a window or two still lit. I looked over my shoulder several times, sneaking a quick glance down each driveway as I passed the small, single-family houses I saw every day. I had walked these streets many times. It was the absolute stillness save for the tap-tap of my steps that had my imagination running wild.

I turned the corner onto my street. My dimly lit front window highlighted my cat's silhouette.

Sweet Meow ran to greet me when I opened the door. Rubbing his soft, warm body against my icy ankle, he purred softly.

"I'm sorry, puss," I said.

I'd neglected him again—said goodbye at six o'clock in the morning and returned at nearly midnight.

But tonight he wasn't angry. He welcomed me home. He deserved a treat. I poured some milk into one dish and some Purina in another. That should garner his forgiveness, and perhaps he would allow me an hour more sleep in the morning, since it was almost Saturday.

Through a fog of fatigue, I reminded myself that I must call Sadie when I woke. I hoped she'd heard from her errant daughter by now. I crawled out of my clothes, and had barely enough energy to wash my face and brush my teeth.

As I tumbled into bed, Big Joe's face flashed before me, leering at me. He knew something about Janice. I was sure of it. What was it he wasn't telling me? I shuddered under the quilt.

Beneath my concern for my friend, however, was the knowledge that I had the weekend off. I wouldn't have to see Big Joe for two whole days.

And maybe Janice would come home, and I could yell at her.

With that consolation, I slept.

CHAPTER ELEVEN

I woke to the clock reading seven-thirty. Without the alarm to wake me, Meow had taken over. He landed on my head. There was only one thing to do—get up and feed my hungry feline.

But yesterday's New York outing was uppermost in my thoughts. I snuggled into the covers a moment longer, smiling. It had been nice. Then my eyes opened wide. *Janice.* I had to find out if Sadie had heard from her.

With a concerted effort, I pushed back the warm quilt and sat on the edge of the bed. Meow rubbed his furry back against my arm, his way of conveying a message. He was blinkin' hungry. I rubbed his back and the top of his head until he purred with delight. Gingerly, I put one foot on the cold floor, then the other. Half asleep, half awake, I must have sat that way for a while. When the telephone rang at eight o'clock, I was still in that unladylike position.

I jumped, grabbed my robe, and ran to the living room, nearly tripping on Meow as he darted out of my way.

I reached for the phone as it rang again. "Hello?"

"Zelda. This is Sadie. I'm sorry if I woke you. You asked me to phone if I heard anything."

"Yes, yes," I said, wide-awake, on edge to hear what she had to say.

"A Detective O'Reilly was here last evening. He asked if I'd heard from Janice. He wanted to know about the man-friend who came calling on her. Janice said he was just a friend. Zelda, what is going on? I couldn't sleep all night, worrying. Why is a police officer asking about my daughter?"

"Have you heard from her?"

"No, I haven't," she said, shattering my hopes. "But if there was something wrong, I would have heard about it. Right?"

I bit down on my tongue. I couldn't find the right words over the phone. There was no gentle way to tell Sadie that Janice was listed as a missing person. She hadn't shown up for work. She hadn't contacted our driver. She hadn't been there for Mary's planned birthday gala. The last time anyone saw her was at the shipyard, three days ago. She had disappeared, damn it.

"Zelda. Talk to me. What haven't you told me? What do you know?" Concern grew in her voice. She was catching on.

I breathed, long and deep. I wasn't about to shout over the phone that no one I spoke to had seen Janice. No one knew where she was.

"Sadie, I'm coming over. I'll be there in half an hour." I hung up the phone before she could ask more questions.

A five-minute shower cleared my head. I had to think about what I would say to console her and Billy. Janice was my best friend. It was time Sadie knew at least as much as I did. Only what did I really know? Nothing.

I put additional milk and some dry food out for Meow, who was already stationed at his lookout post on the windowsill. A cup of instant Nescafe and a piece of stale raisin cake for me, and I was out the door in fifteen minutes, breaking even my record for speed.

As I locked my front door, I reminded myself to stop at the grocer's on my way home. My cupboard was nearly bare.

My car sat at the curb, and I climbed in. I started the motor and let it idle a couple of minutes. This cold weather was rough on cars.

It being Saturday, the roads were fairly empty at this time of the morning. I was at Sadie's in ten minutes, screeching to a stop in front of her building, glad to find a parking spot. I was also lucky no police were strolling about waiting to hand out speeding tickets. I would have been a candidate.

I ran up the stairs, covered the third floor hallway to Sadie's door in record time, knocked, and waited. It seemed like forever until the door opened a crack. Billy stood there looking up at me, tears running down his chubby cheeks.

I hugged him, his small, damp face against mine. His sweet, clean smell enveloped me. "Oh, darling. Please, don't cry. We'll fix everything. Just you wait and see. Where is Gram?"

Billy took my hand and led me to Sadie's bedroom. She was lying across the bed, face down on top of the covers. Oh, my God, she's dead, my mind screamed.

"Sadie," I cried.

Zelda the Welder

I touched her forehead. It was warm. I felt her wrist, felt the beat, slow but steady. She was alive. She had just passed out. I picked up her hand and rubbed it vigorously. I rubbed her arms. I heard a soft moan, but she didn't move.

I couldn't rouse her. I rushed to her telephone and talked to the operator, asking for an ambulance.

Then I waited. Maybe my questions about Janice had frightened her. Maybe she already knew something, but wasn't saying. I could only wait and see. I seated Billy in the kitchen and looked in the icebox. Mostly empty. I wondered at that. Janice always stocked up on milk for Billy. I gave him a slice of bread, and we talked for a while. He told me about his Raggedy Ann.

I checked on Sadie several times. She was still out, but still alive. Her breathing was shallow.

Twenty minutes later, there came a knock, and I ran to open the door. Two men in white jackets nodded to me. Carrying a stretcher between them, the men walked through the apartment. Billy ran ahead, leading them to Sadie. The taller of the men placed a small bottle under her nose.

She stirred, moving her head slowly to one side, her hand coming up to push away the bottle. She coughed and opened her eyes.

"Hi, Sadie," I said.

"What happened?"

The medic answered. "You were out, ma'am. How are you feeling?"

"Dizzy."

"We're going to bring you to the hospital. You'll see the doctor."

Sadie nodded and closed her eyes. Her skin looked waxy, a pale, whitish yellow, the color of new hay.

I turned to the medic. "Hospital? Is that necessary? Won't she be all right?"

"When someone passes out, it's wise to have them checked." He and the shorter man gently placed her on the stretcher.

I picked up Billy and held him close. As the men carried Sadie away, I called, "See you at the hospital, Sadie."

I closed the door after them.

"Gram?" Billy said.

I hugged him. "Don't you worry. I'll take you home with me."

But how could I do that? I had promised to go to a USO dance this evening. I could ask Ida, my neighbor, to watch over him. I owed it to Janice to take care of her son. Besides, I loved the little guy. Besides, there was nowhere else to take him. Besides, I wouldn't leave him with anyone else.

I found a suitcase in the closet and threw in Billy's pajamas, some underwear, a few changes of pants and shirts, and a warm sweater. Then I buttoned him into his warm woolen coat and zipped his leggings. His gloves hung from his coat sleeves on long cords. While he giggled, I held him tight between my knees, pulling the gloves over his tiny fingers, then snapped the flaps of his leather hat under his chin. Suddenly, he pulled away and ran into his bedroom, coming back with a scuffed-up Raggedy Ann under one arm.

All bundled up against the weather, he grinned at me like a tiny tan snowman. I nodded and grinned back. "Where does Gram keep the door key?"

He pointed. It hung on a hook next to the door.

I took it down. "Thank you, Billy."

I gave the apartment a quick perusal. Windows closed. Gas jets off. Lights out. All in order. Picking up the suitcase, I closed the door, locked it behind us, then slipped the key into my purse. I didn't know how long I would be caring for Billy, but I intended to do my best.

We climbed into my cold car. After a minute of pumping the gas pedal, I got the engine to turn over. We drove to Elmhurst Hospital. It was a short ride—just up Grand Avenue and a right onto Queens Boulevard. We wouldn't stay at the hospital long. I just needed to know if Sadie would be okay. Then I needed to get Billy settled at my house. All this change could be unsettling for a little fellow like him.

Janice, come home to your son.

We sat in the waiting room. I held a paper cup of warm cocoa I'd purchased for Billy from the cafeteria. My empty coffee cup sat on a nearby table. One hour and two trips to the rest room later, I caught the nurse's eye for the third time.

"Mrs. Silver is resting quietly. There's nothing you can do here. Please. Go home," she said.

"You *will* let me know if she needs anything?"

"First thing." The nurse nodded and walked on.

Zelda the Welder

I sighed, glanced at my watch, and began buttoning Billy's coat. I slipped his hat on. "We might as well go home and have lunch."

We stopped at the nurses' desk on the way out, and I left my phone number. A solemn expression clouded Billy's face as he looked up. He held his doll in one gloved hand, slipped his other into mine, and we quietly walked from the hospital to my car.

Back at my house, I made us peanut butter and jelly sandwiches. I had some milk left, a half glass, for Billy. Today I had to shop for some healthy kid-food. The stores closed on Sundays.

While Billy ate, Meow inched up to him. Billy tickled my purring pet under his chin. From his finger, he fed the kitty some peanut butter. I could see they had made friends for life. There is something special about children and animals together, a kind of kinship adults don't often match.

After lunch, Billy began rubbing his eyes. I glanced at the kitchen clock. It was nearly one. Time for a nap. I picked him up. Whispering in his ear, I had him giggling and squirming as I carried him to my room. Meow followed. The furry feline jumped on the bed and curled up beside Billy while I took off his shoes and tucked the child in. No more playing sentinel at the window for my pet. This was a far more important job Meow had assigned himself.

Billy turned on his side, Raggedy Ann held close, and was asleep before I closed the bedroom door.

In the living room, I dialed Ida.

The phone rang several times before she picked up. A teary voice answered. "Yes?"

I heard a click at the other end and knew one party line had hung up.

"Ida? This is Zelda. Are you all right? You sound like you've been crying."

"Just listening to the war news on the radio. It's enough to make anyone cry."

Again I heard a click, and knew the other person on our three-party line had hung up. Good. I hated it when they listened in.

"Sorry to disturb you, Ida, but I have a favor to ask. My small friend, Billy Bates, is visiting for a while. He's three. His grandmother was taken to the hospital this morning. I need a sitter for tonight. There's a USO dance this evening. I promised months ago I'd be there for the soldiers. Hate to break my word. Billy showed up on my doorstep, so to speak. How would you like the company?"

There was a long silence at the other end, and I was jittery she would say she couldn't do it. I wouldn't blame her. She was going through a hard time. Every time I walked past her house and saw the gold star in the window, I thought of her pain, of her son who died in Europe.

I heard her blow her nose, heard what sounded like a deep sigh. Then, in a cheery voice, she said, "Yes. I would love to watch Billy. I look forward to meeting him."

"Good. He's a great little kid. Smart, too. Come for dinner. He's napping. When he wakes, I'll introduce you." I paused. "And thanks, Ida." I hung up.

One problem solved. Sitting back in my chair, I contemplated my next move. Working in Jersey had worn thin. I didn't want to climb that ladder again, but I had to check out the shed just one more time. Big Joe gave me the willies. Something about him disturbed me. I still hoped to weld ships for the troops, but I could do it somewhere else closer to home. I recently read an ad in the *Daily News*. Not far from where I lived, a huge warehouse had been converted into an enclosed shipbuilding plant. They made landing barges. They needed shipbuilders and welders. Perhaps I could get a transfer. I'd be practically within walking distance.

While I washed our few dishes, my mind was busy thinking about the change, and the more I thought of it, the more the idea appealed to me. I would call first thing Monday. If Janice wasn't back by then, well, I hoped I wouldn't have to leave Federal before I found out what happened to her. Perhaps Sadie could tell me more about this new man-friend who was "just a friend". I couldn't help thinking this must be how Sherlock Holmes felt setting out on a case. Only finding Janice was not something to jest about.

I'd wait until Ida arrived, then I'd do a quick shop at Gilbert's, the grocery store on the corner. I needed a couple of eggs for Billy for the morning and something for dinner tonight.

In my bedroom, I peeked at Billy, far away in dreamland, his floppy Raggedy Ann snuggled against him. I tiptoed to my closet to pick out what I would wear to the dance.

Zelda the Welder

Ida took one look at Billy, and he at her, and it was love. What she brought with her didn't hurt, either. Billy's eyes widened when he saw the chocolate cake Ida had made for him.

"But only after dinner," she said, placing it on the kitchen counter and smiling at Billy.

"Ida, that's so kind of you," I said.

"I couldn't find a better reason to use my chocolate syrup and sugar," she said.

I knew she had been secreting away rationed sweets for a long time. Today, her eyes had a clearer look, like she'd wakened after a sleep and found that all was not so bad with the world. Maybe she would lose her morbid craving for sugar altogether.

At five o'clock, we sat down to feast on one of my few culinary accomplishments—opening a couple of cans of Campbell's Chicken Noodle Soup. I'd made a big salad of greens and carrots and all things good I could find at Gilbert's, and I had crispy rolls and butter. It would have to do. At least, it was a hard meal to ruin. And

I never met a child who didn't love chicken soup. I wouldn't embarrass him by offering to feed him. He was very bright. I had no doubt he would do us proud.

After chewing quietly for several minutes, Billy swallowed then looked up at me. Spoon clenched in his fist, a somber look in his eyes, he blinked as if ready to ask me something.

"What is it, honey?" I asked.

"Is Gram coming?"

"Oh yes, Billy. As soon as the doctor makes sure she's better. She wasn't feeling so good. Meanwhile, you have Meow, and you have me, and you have Aunt Ida, and we love you, and we'll take really good care of you until your gram is well. Okay?"

There was that look again. "Mommy, too."

I gave him a hug, pushing my face into his soft hair to hide that lump in my throat I was trying hard to swallow. "Your mom, too." I pulled away.

He put on a big smile. "I'm hungry."

"Eat up," I managed, wiping away a tear with the back of my hand.

After dinner, Ida cleared the dishes while I set up a cot for Billy in the spare room I used for storage. I gave him a bath and put on his pajamas. Then I turned on the radio and found WABC. The announcer was just introducing *Captain Midnight*. Billy lay on his belly next to Meow, their legs equally splayed. Who was imitating whom? I wondered, looking at them. They were set to listen to a radio who-done-it.

When Ida came in with slices of chocolate cake, Billy grinned from ear to ear and sat up, one pajama-clad leg crossed over the other.

I watched as he ate the cake, washing each bite down with a swallow of *Ovaltine.* With his ear next to the speaker, his face took on a serious expression. Eating chocolate cake while listening to adventure was serious business.

I wiped away the mustache that lingered from his drink. "Only one show Billy, and then it's time for bed. You and Meow have had a busy day."

I left the three to enjoy their hero. I had to dress for *my* show. I had to be at the dance by seven.

CHAPTER TWELVE

I prepared for my night out. As a volunteer, I showed up for the USO at Clinton Hall every chance I could. I went there to dance with the GIs, some on leave, others soon to go overseas. It was a good feeling, being there for our men who were away from their own homes and families. They were lonely and I was lonely, and it helped to share the pain, perhaps to dance, or laugh, or just sit at a table and talk.

If the weather was accommodating, I walked there from my house, across Grand Avenue and down Maspeth Avenue to Fifty-Eighth Street. Since it was snowing lightly, I would drive tonight.

With loving care, I removed my nylon stockings from the drawer. They were used only on special occasions like this. At the full-length mirror, I twisted to see the back of my legs, adjusting the black line straight down the middle. I hooked the front and back of each stocking to the curved metal latches of my narrow garter belt.

I removed my new red skirt from its royal place in the closet, stepped into it, and pulled up the zipper. It settled in, clinging to my narrow waist, and I swirled around and around, watching the bottom flare out in a wide circle, the hem flying from mid-calf to above my knees.

I paired it with my super-white, frilly blouse. Then I selected black patent-leather heels and a matching handbag. I placed a black pillbox hat over my curls, picked up my black wool coat, and I was ready for my good-deed night. I wanted to wear something to cheer up the boys. Looking in the mirror, I was pretty sure this would do it. I hadn't thought helping them would be good for me, too, but it did improve my tilting ego and put me in a cheerier mood. What had gone on earlier today with Sadie had thrown me off balance.

The ballroom at Clinton Hall was huge. When I arrived, the Mills Brothers were singing *I'm going to find a paper doll that I can call my own…*

The dance floor overflowed with soldiers and sailors and marines, glorious in their dress uniforms. They danced or sat with pretty girls at tables along the perimeter of the dance floor. The girls wore colorful, flaring dresses of every hue. Their hair was arranged in the latest fashions—pulled up high and off the neck or in a pageboy, turned under at the shoulder.

The Hall had an extraordinary history. In the early 1800's, the building was owned by Dewitt Clinton, Mayor and then Governor of New York. Then, for a short time, it was used as the residence of the President of the United States. When the White House moved to Washington D.C., the building stood empty. Much later, it was used for a dance hall and social club. I'd gone to a wedding there once. And now, during the Second World War, it served as a USO, entertaining the troops.

I looked around the Hall, recalling it as it had been. The bandstand remained, with its raised platform and lights. A well-known orchestra performed now. But when I knew it, it was mostly unknown bands or records. The floor burst with teenagers, legs and arms flying. For want of boy partners, the girls danced with each other, mostly the Lindy Hop, sometimes the Peabody. We were on the dance floor for whatever the band played. Once in a while, a young man would ask one of us to dance. Hey, we were fifteen and sixteen, still in high school, pure and innocent.

Occasionally, one of the big bands of the late thirties and early forties played there. I remember standing in front of the bandstand watching a fantastic drummer whose hands moved like lightning bolts. I stood open-mouthed, not moving, watching that man play. His name was Gene Krupa.

There was one unusual evening—I had to smile, remembering. My friends and I had just danced a Lindy Hop and were coming off the dance floor when six young men walked into the Hall. I watched them strut. With a casual attitude, they moved toward our small group, four young ladies laughing together.

I'll never forget how we whispered and giggled when we spotted them. The clothes they wore were different from anything we had seen. Their long jackets boasted broad lapels and wide, wide padded shoulders. Wide-legged pants rode high on their waists and narrowed to tight cuffs at their ankles. Their large-brimmed fedoras hung low over their foreheads, brims turned up. They sauntered toward us, each fellow twirling a heavy, gold-colored chain that went from a belt loop to almost the floor. As they neared, I heard them pop their chewing gum.

One skinny fellow, shorter than the others, swaggered rather than walked. "Hi, girls. Never seen anything like this before?"

"What's that you're wearing?" the girls called out. "Where did you come from?"

The young man shuffled, turning to exhibit his costume. "These are zoot suits, ladies, killer-dillers. They're drape-shaped with reet-pleats, and we're out of Brooklyn, New York, U.S. of A."

I stared, unable to speak.

Then a 78 record of Glenn Miller's song, *In the Mood,* filled the hall. We all started tapping our feet to the beat. One by one, the young men ambled toward us. The skinny one stopped in front of Helen. He twirled the watch at the end of his long chain, and it missed the floor by inches. Holding up his free hand, he bent a finger, indicting they dance.

"Gosh." She giggled. "That would be swell."

Zelda the Welder

Pretty soon, we were taking turns dancing with the zoot-suiters. That night, teenagers that we were, we were thrilled with the aliens in our midst. And they *were* alien to us. They left after a while and never returned. But for months, every time I entered the Hall's vast expanse, for a fleeting moment, I thought of our unusual friends. I saw them standing in a group, chewing gum and twirling their chains.

Tonight, even with the band playing and the dancers swaying to the music of a big time band, they were a more somber lot. Understandably. It was a somber time. The men on the dance floor were part of the war, GIs hoping for a few precious moments when the war could be put aside and life would feel almost normal again.

The uniformed men wore razor-creased pants, fitted jackets, and crew cuts. Some wore shy smiles, like it was their first time away from home. Some, more brazen and daring, laughed and flirted with the girls. They appeared glad to be there, away from the stress of war. I wondered if any of those young men had ever worn those funny *zoot suits* when they were boys, only a few short years ago.

I looked around for someone I knew and spotted Annie, wearing a red polka dot dress and a wide smile. Three Navy officers sat at a table with her. She waved, and I headed her way.

The music started again. At the edge of the dance floor, I was approached by a young Army Corporal. He looked no older than twenty, his face rosy and smooth. He drawled, "Care to dance, ma'am?"

"You bet," I said. "Where are you from, soldier?"

"Texas, ma'am," he replied. There was sadness in his voice.

"I'm betting you miss being away from home."

"That I do, ma'am. My job is with the service right now."

"But your heart belongs to Texas." I tried to make him laugh, and I did bring a smile to his lips, but his dark eyes remained sad.

When the dance ended, a Major tapped my partner on the shoulder, indicating he was cutting in. He was a big, burly, handsome guy with blond hair and the bluest eyes. He looked like more than I could cope with that night.

Zelda the Welder

I brought both GIs to Annie's table and introduced them. We talked and laughed. But the stress of the last couple of days had finally done me in. I left at ten.

CHAPTER THIRTEEN

When I unlocked the door at the reasonable hour of ten-thirty, Ida looked up blearily from the book she'd fallen asleep over. I made coffee, and we munched on the last of the cookies while she gave me a rundown of the shows she and Billy had listened to on the radio. Her eyes sparkled when she spoke of the little fellow.

At eleven o'clock, we said goodnight, and I watched her walk safely across the street and into her house. Then I peeked in on him. He looked like a soft teddy bear. I felt a warm glow of joy. I also felt a deep responsibility for minding him while his family was away.

Closing his door, I trudged off to my own bed to collapse.

Suddenly, daylight broke into my fog of sleep. I jumped out of bed and ran to where Billy slept, tripping on my robe. I hoped to find him still in bed, but he wasn't in the room, and his clothes were no longer on the chair where I had placed them. It all looked surprisingly tidy—the covers pulled up, pajamas crunch-folded and placed squarely on the pillow.

I heard a giggle and followed it to the kitchen. There he was, bent way, way over with his face close to the floor. His tiny fingers tickled Meow's head as the kitty rubbed against him.

"There you are."

Billy stood up. Eyes shining with pride, he held out his hands, wiggling his fingers in front of me. "Look. All clean." He rubbed his hands down his shirtfront. "All dressed."

"Yes," I said, "and a mighty nice job you did, too. Who taught you to make the bed and fold your pajamas so neatly?"

"Mommy." He lowered his head, humble as a boy can be in accepting the praise I had lavished on him. When he raised his eyes again, he wore a more serious expression. "Aunt Zelda." He reached on tiptoe for the top door of my white icebox. There stood a fresh bottle of milk. "See? I carried it."

He closed the door, ran back to the table, climbed onto his chair, and sat.

I couldn't hold back my grin. Not bad for a three year-old—well, almost four. I already knew Billy was a sweetheart, but this topped it all. He was the most thoughtful guest I ever had. For as long as he needed me, this would be his home.

A thought flashed to mind—*I must tell Janice what a good little boy he*—

I closed my eyes, biting my lip. *Where the blazes was she?*

When I opened my eyes, Billy was looking at me, his brow creased in a frown. "Aunt Zelda. Where's Mommy?"

Talk about insight. I leaned forward, lifting his chin so his eyes met mine. "You know, I was thinking, your mom must be having a really good time. Only, she wouldn't want you to worry. I know we'll be hearing from her soon." I hated having no proper answer. I hated what I was really thinking. I hoped I was dead wrong.

I poured a glass of orange juice, which he gulped down like a thirsty child. We both enjoyed a bowl of Cheerios cereal and a cup of Hershey's hot cocoa. Quietly, while Billy played with Meow, I called the hospital about Sadie. They told me she was doing well, but was just then having tests. I could visit her this morning. I hurried to dress in my good black suit with the brass buttons. Then it was time to dress Billy in his outdoor winter gear for a journey across the street.

As we readied to leave the house, Meow sidled up to me and brushed against my leg. He rolled over, and I rubbed his belly. He purred with contentment. He was still my kitty.

That was loyalty. I mussed his fur in a loving so-long-for-now, and he meowed a loud, "Don't be too late coming home." I watched as he ran to his post at the window.

The air was biting, even colder than I expected as we stepped outside. Billy walked beside me, his gloved hand holding mine. He laughed and pointed as our breath made clouds in front of us.

Ida looked up from sweeping a light dusting of snow off her stoop. She swept a lot these days. I understood. It occupied her mind with thoughts of anything but the war and her memories.

Her face lit when she spied Billy. She cooed, "Hello, sweet boy."

"Ida," I said. "What are you doing out here? It's freezing."

Billy let go of my hand and ran to her. "Got cake?"

"I'm guessing you would like to stay with Aunt Ida for a while," I said. "I have some errands to run, and you'll have much more fun with her. We'll get together for lunch. Okay?"

"Okay." He sat on the newly swept stoop. Tilting his head beguilingly, he said, "Kiss Gram, please."

Oh, that child. How did he know I was going to see Sadie? Smart little kid. If I didn't think it would embarrass him, I would grab him and dump a large kiss on that face.

Some kids were playing stickball in the road. Their voices were at a pitch only the young could stand. Little Billy, with his elbows on his knees and chubby fists under his chubby chin, became absorbed in watching the game.

Content that my charge was safe, I left Billy with Ida and crossed to my car, which was parked in front of my house. I would take the short ride to the hospital to see Sadie and find out how long she would be staying.

As I opened my car door, a shadow moved. I looked up. There stood Detective

O'Reilly, wearing his dark fedora and a dour expression.

I felt my stomach lurch, and worked at relaying calm. "Hello, Detective. What brings you all the way from New Jersey?"

"I need you to fill in a few gaps in your story, Miss Bea."

"My *story?* Anything specific?"

"Wednesday morning, when you and your friend, Janice Bates, arrived at the Kearny shipyard, did anything unusual occur? Did she have an argument with anyone?"

He knows something.

I glanced at the small houses lining the street, the windows looking out on us. "Please, Detective. I'd rather not discuss this on the street. May we go inside my house?"

"It would save some time if we got on with it."

I shook my head. I didn't want to remember how I felt when she wasn't on deck to meet me—how I felt when she didn't show all day. "I have nothing to add, Detective. Have you heard something new?"

"Just answer my question, please."

I sighed and leaned against the car, arms folded. "Okay. We warmed ourselves by the fire, then I went toward the DE, and she went to the locker room to get a sweater. She said she was cold. We agreed to meet in ten minutes on top where we were to work that day. She never showed." I shrugged. "As I've said."

He was silent for a minute. Then he asked, "And you are sure she never said anything about seeing someone first?"

"You've asked me three times. Of course, I'm sure. Why would I say so if I wasn't?"

"And you haven't seen or heard from her since?"

I looked at him, puzzled. Where was he going with this? "No, I haven't."

"We found a body in the water—at Federal—close to where the ships are launched."

My heart froze. No preamble. No warning of any kind. How cruel.

"We think it may be Janice Bates. However, the body is swollen, ripped by fish. We need an absolute ID. Her mother is in the hospital. We know you're a close friend. We'd like you to ID the body."

I closed my eyes. I couldn't say no. Janice had been my friend—Janice *was* my friend. Besides, it couldn't be her. I wouldn't have it.

But what if it was?

"I'll go. I have to run across the street a moment to tell my friend I will be longer than I thought. She's minding Billy, Janice's son."

He stood by my car. Without a blink, he said, "I'll wait here."

Ida had been watching us from the stoop. I explained that I had to go with the detective. She nodded and placed her hand on Billy's shoulder. He would be safe with her.

When I returned, the detective took my elbow and directed me down the street to a spanking new, black Ford with those wide, whitewall tires.

They must be paying the law good money these days.

I scolded myself for thinking that way. Why should I doubt Detective O'Reilly? He was one of Jersey's finest. Not a crooked bone in his body. Probably.

He was silent as we rode to New Jersey. Black clouds and dark thoughts chased each other in my mind. I hated death and dead things. I run past cemeteries and never visit a funeral parlor. Yet here I was on my way to view a mutilated dead body dragged from the depths of the Hackensack River. My palms felt wet even inside my gloves.

"Where did they find her... the body?" I swiped at a tear running down my cheek. "Detective... if it should be... her... Billy is such a little boy. He will have to know if his Mom is... I'd rather he didn't know until his grandmother can talk to him. He'll need her support."

He looked at me. "Let's just wait and see if you can identify the body."

The morgue was located in the basement of the local general hospital, one block from the stationhouse. We approached the hospital grounds and pulled around into the emergency entrance. An arrow pointed toward the morgue. We stopped at a pair of large, metal doors at the rear of the red brick building. No one else was parked in this small parking lot. The lot in front of the hospital was crowded with cars and people going about their business. A typical day, only not for me.

Inside the building, we turned down a long, narrow, windowless hall that was dimly lit by low-wattage, overhead light bulbs every few feet. In the movies, morgues were dark, dreary places. Their rooms made one glance around at the shadows and look over one's shoulder. This fit the criteria perfectly. I braced myself to be in the same place as sheet-covered stretchers and drawers in the walls holding even more bodies.

When we reached the end of the hallway, a police officer came through the double doors leading into the morgue itself. He had a stoic expression on his florid face. He instructed us to follow him. The heavy doors closed behind us with a bang.

Though the large room was scrubbed clean and flooded with light, I could only think *this is a place where they keep dead bodies*. I reached for my handkerchief to cut the stench of blood and intestines blending with an obnoxious miasma of cleaning fluid. They tried to disperse the odor of death. Nothing they did could hide the smell. I gagged.

One wall was filled with white, square, metal doors, each with its own small handle. We stopped in front of one such door, second up from the floor. Lips tight, fists clenched, I waited.

An attendant in a white jacket stood near. At a nod from the police officer, he opened the door and pulled out the slab. A low squeal emitted from the sliders, and I shuddered. It sounded like a cry from the cadaver itself. He slid it out and lifted the sheet, uncovering the face. The shadowy outline of the body remained covered.

I breathed into the handkerchief I held over my nose and mouth as I stared at the corpse in front of me. The face of the woman was misshapen and gruesome. Large chunks of skin were missing. What was left was pasty white. The features—the eyes, the nose, even the lips—were purple-black and swollen, but distinct enough to make an identification.

Tears flowed down my cheeks. Amid all that gross, distorted horror, I turned to Detective O'Reilly and smiled. Blood rushed to my face, and I felt faint with relief, but the crease of a smile remained in place.

I wanted to shout, *It's not her. The body under the sheet is not Janice.*

CHAPTER FOURTEEN

We left the morgue and drove the block to the stationhouse. Inside, O'Reilly waved to the desk sergeant. The station was busier than the last time I was there—officers were leaving, others arriving. The glass doors never remained closed for long.

At his private niche in the room filled with desks, O'Reilly pointed to the chair across from his. "Have a seat, Miss Bea."

I sat on the edge of the chair, anxious to be out of there. What more could I offer? I'd done my share of police business and all I could think of was getting home and enjoying the rest of my Sunday.

"Why am I here?" I asked.

The detective sat behind his desk and said nothing, which really irked me.

"Look," I said firmly, "I believe Janice is missing, and I believe not by choice. I have nothing more to add, only that I know my friend. Janice would have sent me a note or told someone to tell me if she couldn't meet me on deck. At the very least, if she were able, she would have contacted her mother by now. So, are you going to find her or not?"

O'Reilly scowled, his face blooming an unattractive purple, obviously unhappy at my outburst. Unpleasant thoughts intruded. What if I were wrong? What if Janice really did run off with a boyfriend? What if she was so irresponsible she would do this and not tell her mother or me or anyone? No, that wasn't Janice. Besides, she knew if she did anything as ludicrous as that and I found out about it, she would wish she were dead.

I picked up my purse and stood, still looking at Detective O'Reilly. On the bookcase behind him, I saw a folded newspaper. It was like a light bulb had been switched on.

—bits of newspaper—the shed atop the DE—torn sheets of newsprint in the wastebasket—

I thumped my forehead with the palm of my hand. How could I have forgotten?

I sat back down. "I am so sorry. This is going to sound silly, but I do know something more. And it might be important. The day after Janice disappeared, I found a note in the pocket of my welding vest. Someone had opened my locker and put it there. The note is at my house. Perhaps when you read it, it will make sense to you. It didn't to me."

O'Reilly sputtered. "You *forgot* to tell me about a note you received relating to Janice Bates' disappearance?"

I nodded. I felt like such a fool. "You see, with Sadie going to the hospital, then having Billy in my care—so much to do. It slipped my mind." I shrugged. "Besides, I couldn't accept what it said, so I set it aside."

"And what did it say?"

"It said Janice was in Miami. There was no name. It wasn't handwritten. Just bits of newsprint put together to spell out sentences."

I waited for a barrage of indignation, but he just sat there looking nonplussed.

I bit my lip, embarrassed. "You'll want to see it." It was a statement, not a question.

Without a by-your-leave, he took hold of my elbow, and with long strides, propelled me across the room. "I'm driving

Miss Bea back to New York," he told the desk sergeant. His tone was crisp and cold.

I had to run to keep up with him. "Hey," I managed.

The ride home was more silent than the ride to Jersey, if that were possible. There was nothing I could say to the man sitting next to me. I had nothing to add, and he likely had more to think about, what with this new wrinkle I just pressed on him.

By three o'clock, we were back on 63rd Street. As we pulled to the curb, I saw Billy and Ida sitting on her stoop. Billy's close-cropped red curls peeked out from around his hat, sparkling in winter's afternoon sun. His large, blue eyes followed some little girls jumping rope next door.

Seeing me, Ida tapped Billy on the shoulder and pointed.

He grinned and waved a greeting. That done, his attention shifted back to the entertainment a few feet from him. I smiled, glad he was enjoying himself. I hoped he'd had his lunch. My stomach cried for food. I'd had nothing since early morning.

As I stepped from the car, Ida stood, brushed off her skirt, and walked across to us. She nodded to the detective, then turned to me. "Billy and I have had lunch, a lovely cheese sandwich and milk and a cookie. We weren't ready for a nap. We decided this was more fun." Her eyes danced, and a big grin lit her face. She had found something to keep her mind busy. I was glad.

Detective O'Reilly stood on the walk. Impatience radiated from his stance. He wanted me to open the house and give him what he'd driven two hours to see.

I told Ida, "We'll just be another few moments."

O'Reilly and I went inside. I indicated a chair for him, but he continued to stand, Fedora sitting rakishly on the back of his head.

"May I see this… note?"

I nodded, and went into the kitchen. From the drawer, I removed the folded bit of paper and handed it to him.

The detective's eyes narrowed. He walked to the couch, sat, and with great care laid the paper on my mahogany coffee table. With the tips of his fingers, he smoothed out the note, stretching it gently so as not to damage the pasted message.

"*Your friend is on vacation in Miami.*" He turned to me. "Does this tell you anything? Does she have family or friends in Florida?"

I shook my head. "None that I know." In my mind's eye, I saw Janice, full of fun, always laughing. One afternoon last summer, we were at Coney Island. I could see her clearly. Her long, red hair flew in the wind, and her sapphire blue eyes, so like Billy's, crinkled as she laughed at something funny I'd just said. Her swimsuit, one of the new styles, was cut high up the thigh and clung provocatively. Boys always gathered around Janice. Maybe she was a flirt, but it was all good-natured fun. "She wouldn't just go to Miami."

I could see O'Reilly's eyes reading me. His whole demeanor changed from questioning police officer to sympathetic cop. Why do they play those childish games, gruff one minute, sweet the next? Did they learn that in police school?

I blew out a breath. "I put the note aside because it made no sense to me. Janice wouldn't go to Miami. I don't believe what it says, Detective."

"I see."

"Also, I have this." I held out the handkerchief with smudges of brown.

"What is it?"

I shrugged. "Dried blood, maybe. I found a trail of it in a supply shed at the top of the DE."

His eyebrows went up. "Any more surprises you forgot to mention?"

"No."

He took the handkerchief gingerly. "Probably somebody just cut their finger, but I'll look into it."

O'Reilly carefully refolded the handkerchief and the note and put them both in his pocket. Patting his jacket, he brought out a small, yellow notebook. He wrote in it, tore off the page, and handed it to me.

It read: *I am in receipt of one newspaper note sent to Zelda Bea and one handkerchief with brown markings.* He'd dated it and signed it with *Detective John O'Reilly*.

I set it on the coffee table. I might need it sometime, though I couldn't imagine why. I didn't want the handkerchief back.

O'Reilly opened the door. He touched his hat with his forefinger in a sort of farewell. "No more surprises. If you hear *anything*, let me know—" he stared down at me, "—*immediately*."

I nodded, closed the door, and leaned against it. *Where do we go from here? Send us a clue, Janice.*

I shivered like—what was the saying—like someone just walked over my grave.

CHAPTER FIFTEEN

After Detective O'Reilly left, I headed for the icebox. I hadn't eaten since breakfast. I pulled out a stale roll and some butter, found some cold spaghetti and one leftover meatball in a covered dish and, not bothering to heat any of it, hastily ate.

I wondered what O'Reilly would decipher from the note. Would he find there *was* someone Janice knew in Miami? I was glad I had given the detective the note. I should have turned it over to him sooner. The old shoulda, coulda, woulda. Now, I had other things to think about, like finding out how Sadie was faring. I sat on the couch and reached for the phone.

The operator intoned, "Number please."

I read aloud the hospital number I had jotted down and waited. There were several rings before I heard a click.

A voice asked, "How may I direct your call?"

"The third floor nurses' desk, please."

"One moment, please."

I waited. Then the phone was picked up.

"May I help you?"

"Yes. I would like to inquire about Sadie Silver."

"Hold on, please."

Several minutes later, I heard a familiar voice. "Hello."

"Sadie. This is Zelda. How are you?"

"I'm well. Much ado about nothing. But they won't let me come home until the day after tomorrow. They want to do more tests on my heart. I hope my angel has been a good boy."

"Billy is fine. He's made friends with my kitty. The cat sticks to him like *Scotch Tape,* thinks he's protecting him. Can I pick you up on Tuesday after work?"

"I'm not sure what time I'll be discharged, so I'll just take a cab. I'll let you know when I get there. Say hello to Billy for me." She hung up.

I blinked and stared at the phone. Sadie was nothing if not to the point. But she was a caring grandmother, dedicated to her small trust. Who was I to complain if she was a little abrupt?

I'd worn my good black suit with the elegant brass buttons down the front, intending to visit the hospital. Of course, I never made it there. I removed my jacket and wrinkled up my nose. Was that the faint odor of the morgue I smelled? I'd be devastated if the suit was ruined.

I hung the suit in my bathroom to air out. Rummaging through my closet, I chose a pleated tan skirt and matching sweater. I would feel more comfortable and I could romp with Billy if I wanted to. I would miss the little fellow once Sadie was home. I wanted him to remember this time as a good time. Suddenly I had an idea. Grabbing my warm fur from the closet, I set out for Ida's house.

I walked in without knocking. Ida and Billy were sitting at the kitchen table drinking hot cocoa.

"Hey, you two." I grinned. "How would you like to see *Bambi*, Walt Disney's new movie? It starts in half an hour. We could walk there. Billy, would you like that? And after the movie, we could go to White Castle and have some of those super wonderful slider burgers." I bent to speak into Billy's ear. "The restaurant looks like a real castle."

"Yay!" Billy clapped his hands.

I turned to Ida. The look on her face broke my heart. I knew she was thinking of her son, perhaps when he was a little boy in a similar situation. It disturbed me that Ida would lose her new friend. There must be something we could do about that.

She blinked, blew her nose, then smiled. "Yes. That would be lovely."

I hustled Billy into his warm coat and his hat that snapped under his chin, and we three set out. We were on the right side of the avenue, walking up Grand, half way to the Maspeth Theatre. As we passed Calverton Cemetery, a long, black hearse pulled slowly past the large, scrolled iron gates. A line of cars entered behind it. Normally I would have run past the cemetery, but I had endured much worse that very morning. Sometimes I was surprised at how brave I could be.

Billy walked between Ida and me. We held his hands, his small fingers incased in the red knit gloves his gram, Sadie, made for him. There was a matching scarf. I had wrapped it twice around his neck, protecting his tiny chin from the cold.

The storekeepers lit their shops early, and their light cut through the early dusk. That afternoon, our town looked like a winter wonderland. Billy laughed each time a trolley car rattled down the tracks. It had snowed earlier in the day, but the constant riding over the rails melted whatever fell there, leaving the path bare, emphasizing the white drifts on either side. One time, Billy giggled and tugged at my hand. I glanced up. The conductor was waving out her small window to get our attention.

Grinning, I vigorously waved back, pointing her out to Ida as the car rattled past. "That's my friend, Ruth. She drives a trolley now. Her husband was drafted. She took over his job until he returns. We women do a lot to keep our world moving." I puffed up with pride. "Oh, by the way, I called the hospital. Sadie will be leaving on Tuesday, if all goes well with her tests. Billy will be going home."

Ida stared ahead. When she spoke, I barely heard her. "Of course. We couldn't expect he would be with us forever. Is she all right?"

"They're checking her heart, but she's feisty as ever."

Ida's eyes welled up. She turned her head.

She was losing her boy again. In this short time, she'd become close to the child. He helped fill that void she lived with since her son was killed. Now she was losing someone dear again. How could I help her? What could I say?

"No reason you couldn't keep in touch with Billy," I told her. "Like a second grandmother, you know. Janice would be pleased. And Sadie is fun. It's time you made a new friend."

Ida nodded, but said nothing.

We reached the Maspeth Theatre. The small lobby was warm and crowded, noisy with excited voices. Children of all ages waited to see the Walt Disney movie. Everyone loved Disney's animated characters. Today they would see a white-tailed fawn named Bambi.

The theatre gave away free dishes to adults. I already had four each of the cups and saucers, and today I received my fourth dinner plate. It had a pretty floral edging of muted greens and reds and browns, with a white center. Of course the dishes weren't bone china, but they would do the job for a start. The expensive china would come later, I was sure.

This new acquisition would go into the hope chest I kept at the foot of my bed. It held two pretty lace-edged tablecloths and some embroidered towels I'd received from a friend. I also had, as a gift from my English mom, a beautiful set of English kitchen knives. They were next to a service for twelve of George Butler's stainless steel flatware from Sheffield, England, and were every bit as pretty as silver. I had refused to buy silver—life was too short to spend time polishing knives and forks. After I married, I would dine happily-ever-after using my acquired set.

I tucked away my thoughts with Ida's and my new dishes in my canvas bag. It was five o'clock, time to start the evening show. With his flashlight guiding the way, the usher directed us to our seats, and we settled in to enjoy the show.

There was a short subject, a cartoon that had Billy giggling throughout. He watched gleefully as a crazy bird fell off cliffs and got into all sorts of mischief as it ran away from a wolf. Then the newsreel, *Movietone News*, came on, and the voice of Walter Winchell, the newscaster, reported the war over film clips of GIs overseas. I gasped at the ferociousness of the fighting scenes and the danger facing our men.

Finally, the theatre quieted as Bambi came on the large screen. Billy sat quite still, his face mirroring his fascination.

"Would you like to live in a forest?" I said.

He smiled up at me, nodding. His chipmunk cheeks were filled with Moon Pie. I had let him take one bite. It would spoil his dinner if he had more.

After the show, we walked out into a cold, moonless night. The air was sharp, and I snuggled Billy's scarf around him. White Castle was four stores down from the movie theatre. The food would fortify and warm us. We devoured sliders and French fries and hot chocolate. While it was not the most nourishing meal in the world for a little boy, once in a while wouldn't hurt. This was our time, and I wanted him to have fun.

By the time we walked home in the frigid weather, Billy was asleep on his feet. Ida carried him into the house. She hummed softly as she removed his coat and gloves and tucked him into bed. Afterward, I made coffee, and we sat together at the kitchen table. I tried to start up conversations about deer and cartoons, but she would have none of it. She just sipped her coffee in silence.

Finally, she said, "What will happen if Janice never comes home?"

"I don't know," I said. "I hate to think about it."

On that cheery note, she said goodnight and walked across the street to her house.

I was cleaning the kitchen when the phone rang. I picked up the receiver and put it to my ear. With my other hand, I brought the mouthpiece close to my lips. "Yes?" I said quietly, so as not to wake Billy in the next room.

"This is Sadie. Where have you been? I've been calling all night. Is Billy all right?"

"Billy's fine, Sadie. You are not to worry. We saw the Bambi movie today. He loved it. My friend, Ida, will watch him tomorrow while I'm at work. I'll bring her to meet you when you get home. You'll like her. And she really loves him."

"I'm so relieved. I had this bad dream. Janice was… was… Oh, Zelda. Please find my Janice."

"I will," I said, wondering how I would keep that promise. "You just relax and do what the doctor says. Okay?"

"Sure. All right. Tell Billy I love him." She hung up, imparting her usual well-chosen words of farewell.

Monday morning, I was awakened before the alarm by the tinkle of the milk bottle placed on the stoop. I reached from my warm quilt and rubbed my sleepy eyes, then sat up.

My sudden movement had Meow skidding off the bed and onto the floor, all in one grand movement. He jumped on the sill and pushed aside the blind to inspect the sudden noise that dared break his slumber.

I peered through the opening. The milkman had moved on, but now the ice truck was outside. I tapped on the window and waved, deciding I had better get a block of ice before he left. I had milk to keep cold for little Billy. He would be with me for at least another night. The iceman nodded in acknowledgment.

I rushed about, straightening my bed and my hair. The doorbell rang. I tightened the belt on my robe as I ran to open the door. The iceman wore a floppy brown fedora and a brown leather vest. He rested a block of ice on a towel on his shoulder.

"Hi, Tony," I said, opening the door wider and pointing to the kitchen.

He knew the way. He replaced the ice in my ice box. I paid him a quarter and, with a tip of his hat, he was gone.

I was about to close the door when I saw Ida crossing the street pulling a small wagon. It was painted red with big white letters reading *Radio Flyer*. The handle was long and black. The tires were large, with yellow caps and black center bolts.

"Look what I found in my garage," Ida said excitedly. "It was my Peter's. I want to give it to Billy. Where is he?"

"Still asleep. Come on in. I'll put the coffee on, and after breakfast we'll surprise him."

I turned to the kitchen doorway. There stood Billy, rubbing his eyes, still in the clothes he wore to bed.

I smiled. "Good morning."

"Hi, sweets," Ida said.

"What's that?" He pointed at the wagon.

"That's a gift for you," Ida said. "Do you like it? All aboard."

A shy smile eased across his face, and he clambered into the wagon.

While Ida rode him around and around the coffee table, I put on the coffee. Good smells wafted through the house. I dressed for work amid the music of laughter and joy. When I returned to the kitchen, all dressed and brushed 'til gleaming, Billy sat at the table with a bowl of Rice Krispies. I had time for a cup of coffee and a slice of toast.

At six o'clock sharp, Jimmy beeped his horn. A quick kiss on Billy's bulging-with-cereal cheek, a pat on Ida's shoulder, and I was off to another day in the Yard.

CHAPTER SIXTEEN

We were used to the ride to New Jersey, and today we made good time. The girls chatted about boys, or laughed at silly things. It didn't seem to bother them that Janice wasn't with us. Was I the only one who was worried?

When we arrived at the Yard, I learned I was assigned to the top of the DE again. I had to finish what I'd abandoned during Friday's snowstorm. I welcomed the news—it would be my last chance to get in that shed. The day was cold, the air clear. All threat of snow had disappeared. The sky was robin's egg blue, an occasional powder-puff of white breaking the symmetry. It would be pretty on deck.

Standing by a fire can warming my hands, I braced myself for what I thought of as Climbing Mount Everest. The climb itself no longer scared me. It was something I was required to do, and I was getting better at it. Of course, if I had my druthers, I would rather be where it was warm, where I could lie in deep green grass, hands behind my head, and do nothing but stare at imagined dragons and castles in the clouds drifting by. I wished I could shut out the world with all its problems. But I didn't have that luxury. I had to find my friend Janice.

Uppermost on my mind was that shed. I had to look for the torn newspapers. They might still be there, and I hoped if I found them, the pieces would fit the letter I'd given Detective O'Reilly.

As I moved from the warmth of the fire, I saw Big Joe. I picked up my gear and started toward the aluminum ladder leading to the top deck of the DE.

Big Joe blocked my way. "Hello, Zelda. Any word from Janice?"

"You tell me. I know you talked to the police before I did, and Mr. Hansen, too. I saw you in his office."

He had the grace to drop his eyes, his mouth forming a weak smile. "Hanson is my boss, too, you know. And I have a job to do. I wish Janice was here doing hers, not off someplace having fun in the sun." Then he pointed his thumb to the DE. "What say we get started?"

Zelda the Welder

Either he was very, very smooth, or he really didn't know where she was. I wasn't sure which.

He was on the ladder directly behind me as we climbed the three stories to the upper deck. It was a long trip. Even though I was getting used to it, I did feel safer with him behind me. My line got tangled once, and he helped me pull it free.

As we reached the deck, I could see workers several hundred feet away. No one was on my end of the huge ship. I set down my bucket and rod and examined the plates I needed to finish. Big Joe stood on the top rung. What was he waiting for? Why didn't he leave? The shed nagged at my mind. With luck they hadn't emptied the wastebasket.

He watched me work with a neutral expression. "Get the job finished today. We're behind schedule."

I pulled on my line to give it some slack. I took out a rod and inserted it. He continued to stand there, staring. I wanted to scream, GO, but I didn't. I wanted to look in the shed, only I couldn't with him there. My frustration built. Abruptly, he started back down.

He disappeared from view. I waited a bit longer before I put down my torch and walked to the shed. The door opened at a touch.

It was dark with lack of windows, but the sunlight streaming in from the open doorway was sufficient to see most of the small room. This was my chance. I may never be working on the deck again.

Someone had been in there since I'd last visited. I recognized the boxes in front, but the back was filled with huge, bulky containers. A yellow rope separated them. I looked for the wastebasket. And there it was. My heart jumped as I moved to it.

I looked inside. It was empty.

"Damn," I shouted, then bit my lip and glanced around, hoping no one outside heard me. Disappointment welled in my eyes. Mission *not* accomplished. I brushed my tears aside and turned to leave. I had no further business in here.

I moved carefully, trying not to stumble over any boxes as I inched toward the open door. In the path of light, I noticed something dark on the wooden floor—a small, square, flat object between two large boxes.

I bent and picked up a leather money purse, like so many others. Except, I knew this one. It belonged to Janice. I gave it to her for her birthday. I'd had it engraved on the back cover. Heart banging in my chest, I held it to the meager light and read the tiny letters. *To my best buddy - Janice Bates - Happy 25.* In front, showing through a square of clear celluloid, I saw a tiny picture of Billy.

She *had* been up here. She'd climbed the DE to work with me. What happened to her?

I tried to clear my head. Janice loved the purse because it fit in her shirt pocket and she could carry it at work. She would never willingly let it go. Had it fallen out of her pocket in a tussle and been kicked aside?

I pulled its zipper. Tucked away were her library card, her driver's license, and her Social Security card. I found loose change, some folded bills—three tens, two fives, and two singles—forty-two dollars. Quite a lot of money for any of us to carry around. If she'd run off with someone for fun in the sun, as Big Joe said, she certainly would not leave her wallet behind. If she'd dropped it, she would go back and find it.

What happened to her?

Tucking the wallet into the back pocket of my jeans, I glanced around once more. It was time to leave. I must not be found here. As I dodged around the boxes toward the open door, a shadow fell over the small room.

Someone stood in the doorway.

My heart leapt to my throat. I sank behind a box, barely breathing. A man walked straight toward where I hid. He pulled the string to turn on the overhead light bulb. Pushing aside some of the boxes, he leaned to read their labels. Then he moved to the bulky containers at the far end of the room and fiddled with the yellow rope.

He was taking so long, I felt my legs cramping. *Find what you're looking for, you fool.*

At last, he lifted a huge, heavy-looking box, placed it on his shoulder, and left, closing the door behind him.

The room went pitch dark.

I knew the area well enough to feel my way forward. I searched for the knob, slowly opened the door a crack, and peeked outside. The man was gone. The area was empty of people. I slipped out. My hand shook as I closed the door behind me.

Whistling softly, I walked away. My heart thumped wildly in my chest. I must show Detective O'Reilly what I found. But first I needed to know if anyone saw Janice. I would ask around again. I had until closing time to find out all that I could, then I would give the purse to the detective. Yes, that was the best plan.

Kneeling at my work, rod in hand, I glanced toward the shed. The man returned to carry out more boxes. I'd barely left in time. I felt myself perspiring even in the freezing cold. I had to focus. There were five short plates left to complete.

I worked fast. No one came near me, and my line performed perfectly. By noon, I was ready to leave. As I bent to pick up my gear, two big, black boots stopped in front of me. I looked up into Big Joe's face not six inches away.

"Hi," I managed.

"Finished?" he said.

My impulse was to shout at him, to push him out of my way. I longed to be on the ground, to walk away from this grinning ape. But I couldn't. Not yet. So, I sighed and said, "Yep. All done. I'm ready to call it a morning."

"I saw you." Big Joe's voice became a feral growl. He wasn't smiling now.

"What?"

"The shed. I saw you come out of the shed. What were you doing in there?"

Without thinking, my hand went to my back pocket. As casually as I could, I continued to gather up rods and bucket, shield and brush from the floor. "What was I doing in the shed? That's a silly question. What does one do in a shed?"

"You tell me. I came up to ask you something, and you weren't working. Then I saw you leaving the shed. So, again, what were you doing in there?"

My mind raced. Think, girl, think. I forced a smile and a roll of my eyes. "Is it off limits? Sorry. I was just looking for the *Ladies*. I thought it might have a toilet."

He seemed to deflate at my explanation. "If you really need a john, there's one at the far end of the deck where the men are working." He reached for my elbow. "I'll show you."

I pulled away. "No thanks." My face felt hot with my lie as I stood looking up at him. "I've finished. I'm going down."

He didn't move. A sick sort of grin spread over his face. I wished I could swat him like a fly and get him out of my way.

He took a moment to peruse the work I'd just completed, and nodded. "Nice job." He raised his brow. "Hey, I brought up some lunch. I'll share it with you. We could, you know, relax and enjoy the view."

Lunch? My stomach turned. "Why, thanks, Mr. Morgan. But I promised the girls I'd lunch with them if I finished my work up here."

"I'll be the judge of that. I can give you more work if that's what it takes."

There was that smirk again. He was flirting with me. The man was a wolf. I wouldn't be surprised if he grew fangs and howled at a full moon. But he'd lied to me, and I was convinced he knew where Janice went. Nobody lies for nothing. This may be my only time to find out what he was hiding. I had to make him think I liked him. Then perhaps I could pick his brain, see how much he wasn't saying. In the time it took to shoulder my tools, I convinced myself that having lunch with Big Joe was the right thing to do.

"I've never picnicked this high in the sky before," I said with a coy smile. "It might be fun."

His face went blank for a second, and then he grinned wider. "Just like all dames. Can't make up your mind."

I shrugged, hoping I hadn't raised his hackles too much, or anything else. He turned, his lunch box dangling from his hand, and beckoned to me to follow him. When I caught up, he led me to a spot at the railing. It overlooked the waterways. Tiny waves rippled onto the shore of the wide Hackensack River. Completed ships swayed and bumped in their slips. I could see the tiny figures of the workers moving around the vessels. Lines of flags flapped gently. The sun shone overhead like a huge yellow ball floating in a pale blue field. There was not a cloud in sight. But for the bitter cold, I might think it was a day in spring.

"This view is spectacular," I said.

I wrapped my floral silk scarf closer around my neck, freeing it from my jacket. The thing about wearing silk as opposed to wool was twofold for me. One, the wool tickled my skin and itched, and two, the silk was female identity, a contradiction to the sterile, male garments I wore on the job. Today, as a soft breeze played, I let the light fabric flap and dance. It stretched out to tap Big Joe as he stood next to me. The scent of my Chanel N°5 perfume floated on the air. How else to lure a man to confess but to spice up a bit of femininity?

He brushed the cloth away, snapping, "Stop it. You girls are all alike. Bates played that game with that damn animal scarf of hers."

My mind raced. Janice teased him with her scarf? She never mentioned flirting with Big Joe. She never flirted with any of our male co-workers, much less the boss. The only man we were overtly friendly with was Otto-the-cop, and that was because he'd have none of it. It didn't make sense.

Big Joe reddened as if ashamed of his outburst. His voice turned soft. "How about some food? I brought coffee."

I forced myself to relax. "Great."

From his lunchbox, he brought out a thermos of coffee, filling the small red cup for me. He drank from the container. Then he took out a paper-wrapped submarine sandwich. Tearing the paper in two, he handed me half.

I gawked at the long roll. It was stuffed with cold cuts and cheese and lettuce and tomato and onion and olive oil and vinegar and seasonings, and I wondered how on Earth I was supposed to wrap my mouth around the monstrosity. There was enough food for four people from my half alone.

I made a valiant try to bite a corner of the sub, trying to hold it together with both hands as the contents slid out the bottom. I looked over at Big Joe. He was munching away, obviously enjoying his half. I set the sloppy mess onto the paper and sipped the coffee. It was overly sweet and had a strange tang. Had he spiked it? Did he drink his coffee this way all the time?

"Thank you, Joe. This is nice. Did you bring it from home? Did your wife make it for you?"

"I don't have a wife," he drawled, looking through half-closed eyes at me. "So." He chewed, swallowed, then said, "Do you enjoy working at Federal?"

"I like doing my part. I gave up a good job to do this."

His eyes swept over me. "I'm sure glad you did." There was that leer again, like he would like to munch on me along with his sandwich.

"Tell me," I asked, "how come you're not in the service?"

His eyes burned into mine as he spat out, "What I do here is important."

Blood flooded my face. I nodded. "It is. It is. The men couldn't fight without ships. Someone has to build them." My hand went out to pat his. He pulled away. "I only meant that you're a well-built man. You look in your prime."

He didn't answer for a moment, then, "Drop it. Okay? Just drop it."

"Sure." I picked up a bit of bread and attempted another nibble. "I bet you didn't know this is my favorite food. Janice's too. The girls and I sometimes stop at Dominic Conti's grocery store. It's on the way home, on Mill Street, in Paterson. Know the place? They're famous for their submarines. Navy food." I chuckled. "This is as good as theirs any day. Janice will be sorry she didn't stick around."

He cast a sidelong glance my way and moved in closer, his arm touching mine. With his voice several octaves lower, he said, "Hey, are we going to talk about Bates all day? She isn't even here. I'd rather talk about you."

"I only meant that if she could be here she would love it. Where exactly did you say she went?"

"I didn't." His jaw tightened. He moved away, squashing his waxed butcher paper and shoving it into his lunch box. "Finished with the cup? I have things to do."

Well, so much for that. I wasn't very good at this private eye business. I hadn't even chanced the important questions. Gathering my uneaten lunch, I folded everything back in the paper. Unobtrusively, I let my coffee tip out and over the rail. I handed the empty cup and wrapped submarine to him. I'd put my foot in my mouth along with an unhappy lunch. He'd given me nothing. Now there was nothing I could do but leave.

"Well, that was lovely," I said. "Thank you. I'll go down now. There must be work for me below."

I felt his eyes on me while I walked off. As I stepped over the edge and onto the ladder, I looked up and saw him turn away. Before the top of the deck disappeared from my view, Big Joe had walked to his workers at the other end of the DE. He said something, and the men glanced my way. I heard laughter. What was he telling them? What was he implying? Whatever it was, it showed every time he looked at me. He lied about Janice—of that I was sure. And what of the shed? He yelled at me for being there. What did he think I'd find? The fury he directed at me was more than just about Janice. He bought the ladies room lie, but what had made him so upset in the first place? What was he so afraid of? Those were the answers I wanted. My hand went to my pants pocket, and I felt the bulge of the small purse.

CHAPTER SEVENTEEN

Now I knew something bad had happened. Janice's purse held all her cards plus Billy's picture. She would have gone back and searched for it. If she could.

I have your purse, Janice. You knew I'd be looking. Where are you? Help me find you, damn it.

Detective O'Reilly was my main hope. I would tell him what I'd found, but first I would ask around in the yard one last time, perhaps get a few answers.

At the nearest of the blazing fires, several welders huddled together. Even their heavy denim, their lined jackets and suede vests weren't enough to keep them from the winter's chill. They stood around a coal-burning tin barrel. The sun had disappeared behind a suddenly overcast sky, and as the afternoon grew, each hour turned colder. Too cold even for snow.

But I felt the heat of frustration. I wanted to scream to the people warming themselves, *Do you know where Janice Bates is? Do you have any idea what has happened to her?*

I approached, and they looked up as if I had called to them. My gaze took in the mixed group. They were mostly female—young, unmarried, a few older women, wives, and mothers. There was one man, Jake Steinman, a heavyset man past his prime, and a few boys who came in after school. They contributed their time here.

I rubbed my hands over the warmth rising above the fire and greeted them with a moronic, "Hear anything interesting lately?"

Nice start, girl. Is that the best you can do?

Voices murmured in greeting, but nothing to help me find Janice. I wasn't going about this correctly.

Thrusting out my chin, exhibiting all the authority I could muster, I addressed the group again. "Folks, I need your help." They stared, waiting. I took a deep breath. "Janice Bates is missing. Last Wednesday, she was supposed to be working with me over there on that destroyer escort." I pointed over my shoulder. "Janice and I were to meet on deck three. She didn't show. She hasn't been seen or heard from since we arrived that morning. She hasn't been home to her little boy, and her mother has received no messages from her. Is there anything anyone can tell me? Anything you might have seen or heard last Wednesday? Something that struck you as strange?"

No one spoke.

Then one tiny voice piped up—Sue Carroll's. She welded with us sometimes. "I saw Janice going up the ladder that morning. But not the main ladder. It was the other one. By the painters."

"Was anyone with her?"

"No, she was alone. I waved to her, but she didn't see me. She seemed to be in a hurry. Sorry I couldn't be more help."

"Thank you, Sue. Every little bit of information helps."

"Miss Zelda?"

I looked around. "Rusty?"

It was one of our young students who filled in after school, a short, thin boy, about sixteen. He was jumping from one foot to the other, smacking his arms. He stopped long enough to raise a gloved hand. "I remember somethin'. I was deliverin' some rods 'round the other end last

Wednesday. I saw Mr. Morgan comin' down the far ladder. He was carryin' a duffle bag. When he got to the ground, he set it down real easy like. At the time, I wondered what he had in it to be so careful, then I forgot about it."

My throat caught. *No. It wasn't possible.* "Did you see where he went?"

"Yep. He walked on through toward the parkin' lot carryin' the sack."

He brought down a sack, stashed it in his car. No, no. Ludicrous to think it could be a body. Janice's body?

I smiled through my fears. "Thanks, Rusty."

I looked away to stare into the fire, terrible thoughts swirling in my head—scary, frightening thoughts, like Big Joe catching Janice in the shed, fighting her, knocking her out, hiding her in the bag. What had she seen him doing in that shed?

Mr. Steinman, the older gentleman, broke into my thoughts with a chuckle. "That reminds me of the story of the wheelbarrow." He spoke in a clipped, New York accent, spreading out his hands, gathering heat from the fire. "At the end of each day, this worker wheeled out a wheelbarrow loaded with dirt. One day, the guard at the gate stopped him and asked what he had in the wheelbarrow. Just dirt, the man said. The guard sifted his fingers through the mass, and found it was only dirt. Okay, the guard said. Each day he checked then waved the worker on. He never figured out the man was stealing wheelbarrows."

Laughter followed.

Someone called out, "Perhaps Big Joe Morgan was stealing something from the Yard."

"Or he was carrying home his dirty laundry," I said, repeating Big Joe's reply to me when I'd asked.

Would they think I was crazy if I said he'd had Janice in the bag?

The workers ambled away. I remained by the fire, hands tucked in my armpits as I bent toward the flames. The sky became more overcast with every passing minute. "Damn, where's the sun? Isn't it going to warm up today?" My head pounded with a greater question.

Where the hell was my friend?

I heard a clearing of the throat and looked around. Big Joe stood behind me. He beckoned with his forefinger. I followed.

Zelda the Welder

He pointed to a weld on a flat sheet of metal. It was badly done, all bubbly with deep, open spaces. I didn't look to Joe for instruction, just set down my bucket and got to work. I never wanted to speak to Big Joe again. My wire brush broke up and pushed away the bad weld. I wondered who had done such a poor, sloppy job as I burned out the beaded section and replaced it with a neat, clean bead. By the time I finished, Big Joe had left.

I headed back to the fire. As I walked along, I heard Frank Sinatra singing, *I'll never smile again, until I smile at you.* I glanced around. The music was soft, yet it filled the air even over the sounds in the yard. Someone must have one of those Zenith portable radios everyone was talking about. The sound was like magic, right there in the open. I listened, and the shipyard melted away. The song was sad. The soft melody drifted past the tall ships anchored nearby. The water slapping at their sides kept time as they swayed with the wind and tide.

I was reminded of the last time Janice, Mary, Annie, and I went to a USO dance at Clinton Hall. Duke Ellington's band played *Don't Get Around Much Anymore.* We were consoling one another, remembering the men we knew and loved, far away somewhere overseas locked in a nasty war. Now my friend was gone, and I didn't know where.

As I walked on, the music faded. I glanced at my watch. It was four-thirty. I was eager to get home to see little Billy, but perhaps I should stop at the hospital, visit Sadie for a short while. I felt a tap on my shoulder and jerked around.

Big Joe Morgan stood there. I took a deep breath. It was now or never. Looking up at him, I said, "Mr. Morgan, I'm really concerned about Janice Bates."

"Are we on that again?" He grinned, more like the Cheshire cat than an amused man. "She's probably in Miami soaking up the sunshine while we freeze our backsides off. We're the ones to feel sorry for."

His gaze swept over me, and I wanted to take a bath. My hand went to my mouth, holding back several foul words.

"Hey," he said, his eyes lighting up, "how would you like to go to Florida with me? We could look for Bates together. There are lots of fun things to do down there. They say the sun is always shining on those sandy beaches."

Here, the sun hid behind encroaching gray clouds, and a mean wind whipped my scarf across my face. Big Joe stared down at me, trying to make me believe that Janice just up and left for a fun vacation.

I was about to say something I knew I would regret later, when the whistle blew. Time to quit for the day. The night crew flowed in from the parking lot. I forced a smile as I turned from him, waving good-bye. I didn't look back.

The sooner I got home, the better. It would be great to clear my head of all that went on today. I didn't like asking questions, picking at minds, getting limited answers. I didn't like fighting the boss. It felt like he was trying to keep me quiet about Janice.

What did he really know? He was always at my back, ready to jump, more than a foreman should. It was clear he knew *something*. He joked, claiming to know where she had gone. He wanted me to believe she would tell him and not tell me.

Well, if I believed anything, it was that there was more he wasn't saying. And I had nothing concrete to go on except this damn nagging feeling.

I shook my head, fighting to get Joe Morgan out of my thoughts. No more tonight. It was time to go home and see sweet little Billy.

CHAPTER EIGHTEEN

Cars roared from the parking lot—day workers anxious to get home to their families and warmth. Ahead, I saw our driver, Jimmy, busily polishing every inch of his love, the Imposing Buick.

Catching up to Mary and Annie, I grabbed their hands and pulled them along, yelling, "Come on, girls."

We hailed Jimmy. He looked up and waved back, a big grin creasing his plump cheeks.

We reached the Buick. Many of the cars had already left. As I started to climb into the back of the car, my eyes swept the large, open area around us. I froze.

There, one lane ahead in his allotted parking space, Big Joe Morgan was leaning his skinny ass against his fancy black Lincoln. His whitewall tires shone in the setting sun as, legs and arms crossed, he stared at me across the space. This time he really did scare me.

I turned and flopped into the back of Jimmy's car. "Let's go. I'm ready when you folks are."

The car rumbled into gear, and we slowly moved out. Heaving a sigh of relief, I turned and looked out the back window. Big Joe was still there, staring after the car. Only he wasn't smiling.

The evening traffic was heavy as we passed through New York. At the Hudson Tunnel, we had to wait in a line. The ride through Long Island City was uneventful, however. More than two hours later, Jimmy dropped me off at Ida's house to pick up Billy.

I waved to Jimmy and the girls from the curb. "See you tomorrow."

I ran up the steps of the immaculate, scrubbed stoop and rang the doorbell. Inside, the radio played—the new Majestic her son bought her before he left for the war. Did he sense he was never to return and wanted to leave her a memory?

I brushed the thought away, happy to see a cheery, much more relaxed Ida greet me at the door. Beaming, I peeked into the living room. Billy was in his pajamas, his face all shiny and clean. He lay on his belly in front of the radio, his chubby legs raised behind him, elbows on the floor, chin in his small hands. The William Tell Overture blasted the room. Then came the pounding of horse hooves, and I heard the voice of *The Lone Ranger* say, "Hi-ho, Silver. Away." Abruptly, the announcer broke in to talk about *Silvercup Bread*.

"Hey, Billy," I called. He twisted toward me, his face locked in a mask of concentration. "Hey," I laughed. "This show is the greatest." I walked over, gave him a hug, and ruffled his curls. Then I plopped into one of the stuffed chairs flanking the radio. "Let's see what's happening."

Ida came into the room bearing gifts. She handed me a tray of food, then sat in the chair on the other side of the radio. I blinked at her. "This looks wonderful. But what about you and Billy?"

"We've already eaten," she said. "He did very well, our little boy." There was a glow about Ida I hadn't seen in a long, long time.

"Thanks." I stuffed her homemade bread and delicious cabbage soup into my starving mouth. I hadn't eaten for hours. It tasted better than any nectar made for the gods. As I mopped the last of the soup with the last of the bread, I looked up. The end of my dinner coincided with the end of Billy's half-hour radio show. "This was the best meal ever, Ida. Just what I needed to get over a bad day." I glanced toward the little fellow. "Have you heard anything from his grandmother? She promised to call and let us know she was coming home."

"Not a word. Why don't you call the hospital?"

"I will as soon as I get Billy home. It's bedtime."

We crossed the street to my house. Once inside, I locked the door and stooped to help Billy take off his coat.

A serious little boy stared up at me. "Aunt Zelda… One more show… Please?"

I looked at the clock on the mantel. It was seven-thirty. "And what show is that?"

His eyes lit, a smile turning his sweet face rosy pink. His high-pitched three-year-old voice made the sound of a squeaky door, followed by a deeper, "What evil lurks? The Shadow knows."

I couldn't hold back my laughter. After that display, how could I say no? "Wow, you scared me. It is kind of spooky."

Billy giggled. "Gram lets me."

"Okay, if you say so. But after the show, it's straight to bed."

He nodded and hugged my legs, then ran to my Emerson and turned it up high. For the next half hour nothing was heard but the projected sounds in an unwinding tale of good over evil.

The announcer signed off, and I switched off the radio.

After he brushed his teeth, Billy went to his room. He knelt, clasping his small hands before him, and in a clear voice recited, "Now I lay me down to sleep." I swallowed a clump of tears as he prayed. I made out, "Let Mom come home. Gram, too. Take care of Aunt Zelda and Aunt Ida." The words were jumbled, but I'm sure God knew what he said.

Wearing a contented smile, a sleepy little boy climbed into bed. By the time I'd tucked his covers around him, he was asleep.

Although Billy was not my child, it was getting harder to accept he wasn't as much a part of my family as Meow, curled now at Billy's side. Before he had jumped on the bed, Meow had rubbed his soft body against my legs to assure me he was there and ever vigilant.

I threw a kiss to both of them, then closed the door gently.

After changing into my robe and slippers, I prepared a cup of tea. I blew on it and took a sip. With cup in hand, I returned to the living room. It was already a few minutes after nine. I wanted to talk to Sadie before they closed the ward for the night. I lifted the earpiece and rang the hospital. The switchboard picked up immediately.

"Is it too late to speak to a patient?" I asked the cheery voice at the other end.

"What name, please?"

"Sadie Silver."

"I'll see if she is awake. Hold on, please."

Minutes later, I heard, "Hello. Hello. Anyone there?"

I jumped at the loudness, holding the receiver away from my ear. "Sadie, I hope I didn't disturb you. It's me, Zelda. I'm sorry I didn't get by to see you tonight. I was late getting home. Do you know when they will let you leave?"

"Not just yet. They want to keep an eye on my blood pressure. Another day or two, they say. When they get their hooks into you, they don't let go. How's my boy?"

"He's fine and fast asleep. He listened to his radio shows and was out before the lights were turned off. He's such a good little fellow, Sadie. You have done well. Tell me, have you heard from Janice yet?"

It was quiet on the other end. Then she said, "No. But she'll be home soon. I know my girl. You'll see."

I heard a tremor in her voice. She was putting up a brave front, but I could tell she was more than a little concerned. "You're right. I know we'll hear from her in a day or two."

"Sure. Well, nice talking to you. Give my love to Billy." I heard a click. She'd hung up.

As I slipped the receiver back onto its cradle, I reminded myself I would need to rise-and-shine earlier with Billy in my care. I shouldn't be awake and wandering around the house. Still, sleep eluded me. I needed a quick fix. In the icebox, I found the last of Ida's chocolate cake, enough to go with my cooled tea.

I turned on the radio. CBS anchor Douglas Edwards of *The World Today* was on the nightly news. Current events carried the war on both fronts. In retaliation for a German attack, our planes dropped so many bombs on the city of Dresden it was destroyed. On the other side of the world, the Japanese war was becoming desperate. We were losing men and planes and vessels and islands. In the past, our country had lost many battles, but never a war. As I switched off the radio, I prayed it wouldn't happen on our watch.

I pushed the half-eaten cake away, my appetite lost. The phone rang, and I reached for it. "Yes?"

"Hi, hon. It's me, Mary. Have you been listening to the news? There's a war bond drive this weekend, and they're crying for volunteers. I think we should check it out. They mentioned some big names. Interested?"

"Mary, take a deep breath and start at the beginning. Where are they holding it?"

I heard her tinkling laugh through the wires. "The Hall."

I contemplated the prospect for a moment. *Anything for our boys. Either Ida will watch Billy or Sadie will be home.* I raised the mouthpiece. "Mary—"

"I understand. You've been in a stitch since Janice went missing. This is a bad time."

"No. I want to help in any way I can. Let's do it. Sign me up. Will Annie be going, too?"

"I hope so. I'll call her," Mary said. "Have you heard anything from Janice?"

"No one has heard anything. Not Sadie, not the police, and certainly nothing from our engaging boss, except to tell me to lay off and stop asking questions. I'd like to pick that big oaf's brain, provided he has one. Do you think he knows more than he says?"

"Maybe. There *is* something slimy about the man. Be careful, huh?"

"I intend to be."

CHAPTER NINETEEN

A ringing woke me. Turning over onto my stomach, face buried in my pillow, hands holding my ears, I squeezed my eyes tightly closed. It couldn't be time to get up. I wasn't ready. I wanted these last moments.

The ringing kept on. Lifting my head, I squinted into the morning light.

Slowly, I pulled my arm out from the warmth of my eiderdown quilt and reached to end the pesky sound of my alarm clock.

The clock read ten minutes to five—ten precious minutes left of sweet slumber.

My eyes flew open. It wasn't the clock. It was the telephone. Who would call me at this hour? *Janice...*

Let it be good news, I prayed, rolling out of bed and bumping my *derriere* on the floor in my haste to reach the phone before it stopped ringing.

I stood up, tripped twice, then struggled into my robe as I ran to the living room and grabbed for the receiver. I dropped it, caught it by its long cord, lifted it to my ear, and managed a "Hello?"

"Zelda?"

"Who else?" My voice crackled.

"I'm sorry. Jimmy here. We have a problem. My car won't start."

I felt the blood beginning to flow again as I came back to life. Then realization hit me. "Oh… But we have work… Can you get it fixed?"

"'Fraid not right away. It will kill the morning. I have a great big favor to ask. Can you use your car to pick up the girls and drive to Jersey today?"

"Of course. I'll call Annie and Mary."

"Knew I could rely on you. We can't all stay home and wait."

"I never drove that far before. Hope I have enough gas."

"When you get there, ask for gas stamps at the office with the timecards. They help out if you need it."

I rubbed my eyes and rotated my shoulders. "Want me to pick you up also?"

"I'll drive to Federal as soon as my car is ready."

"Okay. See you later, then."

I replaced the receiver. I had to check on the little guy. It was getting late if I was to pick up the girls.

I shouldn't have been concerned. Billy was sitting up in bed with Meow, his chubby cheeks flushed, giggling and having a grand old time.

"Hey, fella'. I see you're ready to start the day. Dressed and breakfast in five minutes."

"Okay." He grinned, jumping from the bed. "Meow," he called as he ran to the bathroom, "brush teeth."

I felt a pang of love and sadness. I was going to miss Billy when he returned home.

After I worked out the change in plans with the girls, the rest of the early morning hour went along nicely. I placed Billy with Ida and waved goodbye to Meow.

I picked up Mary then Annie. I felt good about myself. Here I was driving through the Holland Tunnel out of New York City and on to Kearny, New Jersey. It was easy. I made the trip so many times with Jimmy. Heck, I built ships. I was a worker on the finest vessels in the world. Driving a car was simple.

"We're lucky I haven't had to drive much this week or I wouldn't have enough gas," I said.

"How will we get home without gas?" Annie asked.

"Jimmy said Federal will give me added rations if needed."

"Good," she said, the relief evident in her voice. Annie was the alarmist in the group.

The yard was nearly filled by the time we got there, but our luck held—Jimmy's usual spot near the front was still open. I made for it. As I pulled in, I saw Big Joe leaving his car, parked close to our spot. Willy, another foreman, sauntered up to him. From their gestures, they got into what seemed a heated conversation as they walked toward the entrance. They didn't look our way.

Thank you, God. I wasn't in the mood for his smartass remarks just then. I was grateful he hadn't seen us arrive.

I glanced down at my gas gauge. Close to empty. My B classification for gas rationing allowed me eight gallons a week, but that was only because I worked at the Federal Shipyard in New Jersey and lived on

Zelda Becht

Long Island, New York. The job got me four more gallons a week than I would have had with an A classification. I counted myself fortunate. I saved my gasoline for other uses because Jimmy drove me to work. I had driven the posted thirty-five miles an hour and it got us here, but now there wasn't enough left to get us home again.

I turned off the ignition. "Let's go to work, girlfriends."

We grabbed our lunch pails from the back seat and hopped out of the car. On a whim, I detoured to Big Joe's car. Mary called to me, but I waved her on. This was where Rusty thought Big Joe put that bag.

I wished I could open the blasted thing. And what would that prove, anyway, except that he drives a shiny black Lincoln? He must make a lot of money to afford an expensive car like this.

I walked the length of the car, my fingertips trailing its long, clean lines. It was backed in, nose to the front, the rear facing the fence. I noticed something sticking out. I leaned closer. There was a piece of... cloth? It was two inches long, barely discernable as it lay against the black of the car, a tiny swatch of brown and black print peeping from the closed lid of the trunk. I stared closely. Touched it. It was silk.

Janice's leopard scarf?

I pulled on it, hoping to get the whole scarf out, but it tore as it caught in the trunk lock. I took away a piece of fabric about six inches long. I began to shiver. I couldn't stop. I held myself tight, trying to stay calm. I slumped to the ground behind the Lincoln, clenching the torn piece to my chest, rocking back and forth like I held a baby in my arms.

After a minute, I calmed down. This proved nothing. He could have picked up the scarf as it lay on a table or on the ground and tossed it into his trunk. He could have taken it from her. Or he could have found one similar to the one Janice bought.

But I knew that print. I knew it well. I knew most of Janice's clothes. We shopped together. We had both wanted the unusual animal print, and we teased over who would get to buy it. She won.

Burning in my thoughts was a grinning Big Joe when I asked him about Janice.

And as I sat there, an idea clicked in my brain. But I had to work it out. It was only doable if Jimmy came to work today so he could drive the girls home. But now I had to move. I needed that gasoline. I needed a plan. I tucked the bit of cloth into my pocket and ran to catch up with the girls.

"Where have you been? We were about to go back for you," Annie said.

"I was just looking over some of the cars. Listen, girls, I have an errand to run this afternoon. Jimmy said he would be here as soon as his car is fixed. He will be able to take you home."

Mary looked quizzical. "And where would you be going?"

"First, I have to see if they give me the gas Jimmy promised. Funny thing about this gas rationing," I said, trying to appear flippant while I changed the subject. "I read somewhere it's the rubber in our tires our government is concerned with saving, not the gasoline. The Japanese armies in the Far East cut off our biggest supply of rubber."

"I guess those bureaucrats in Washington *are* doing their job," Annie said. "Who knew?"

"Whatever," Mary mumbled, putting on a big smile as she waved to a couple of women passing. "You still haven't told us where you're going."

Zelda the Welder

We entered the small office with the timecards.

"Go on ahead," I said. "Cross your fingers Jimmy's right or my car is stranded in New Jersey until next week's rations."

I could hear them giggling at the likelihood as they walked on.

Avoiding Otto's glare, I handed the girl at the desk my driver's license and my ration card. She gave me a form to fill out and a small map for the location of the gas station. I had never been anywhere in the Yard but the large section where I worked. Federal was miles around. The gasoline pumps were nearby, and there would be only a minimal charge for the gas. I could drive my car over later in the day.

"Thank you," I said, taking a deep breath of relief. Despite what Jimmy had said, I had been concerned I might *not* get the gasoline. And I needed it if I wanted to carry out the plan formulating in my mind. Now I could concentrate on my next move.

As I pushed the folded permit into my rear pocket, my fingers touched the bit of silk cloth.

CHAPTER TWENTY

I was to work ground level today. Slip seven. A new vessel was waiting in its berth. Gathering my bucket and a supply of rods, I walked to my assignment on the look out for our foreman.

I liked placing the sparking rods to the cold metal sheets. I liked watching the melding of two pieces of steel into one, the bead pure and straight, freezing into tiny waves. I liked knowing my work would become part of a strong, safe ship that would carry our servicemen across the seas. It was a good deal more rewarding than typing legal papers in a sterile office.

But no one, not Mr. Big himself, could make me climb that open-air ladder again. It wasn't the climb I was afraid of most—I'd almost become used to the trip. I was more frightened that our grinning foreman would be there, so far away from everyone. It was a long way down. Pretty horrible thought, that.

But there were other things troubling me. After finding the piece of silk, I knew Joe Morgan was hiding something. He seemed smitten with Janice. Perhaps he took the scarf from her as a keepsake, then tossed it into the trunk of his car—or perhaps it got there with its owner. The latter I knew to be a stretch, but the thought wouldn't go away. She was missing. There were *no* answers. And I didn't trust him.

The Kearny Shipyard was active this morning. Celebrities were expected. I was working one slip over from where a finished vessel would be christened with champagne and sent down its way, prepared to sail wherever the wars took it. And here I was, near enough to witness my first launching ceremony.

In war, ships were finished daily and sent to sea by the hundreds. So many ships slid down the ways, it was not possible for all of them to have ceremonies. Time was an important factor. But this ship would have the distinction of having First Lady Eleanor Roosevelt doing the honors.

The Yard buzzed with excitement. I knew once the ceremony began, my fellow welders would stop work to line the walk for a quick peek at our distinguished guests. From where I was positioned, I could see the bustling workers readying slip eight for the morning's festivities. Next to the ship, a wooden platform had been erected. It was draped with American flags. A band of musicians waited there. They looked cold. On the ship, small, triangular flags had been strung on long ropes from stem to stern, fore and aft. The air was frigid, but the breeze off the water was slight, gently ruffling the colorful red and white bits of cloth. The name of the vessel being honored was newly painted on its side—the *USS BLUE RIDGE*. They were making an occasion of it. I was pleased to be a witness.

At ten-thirty, three elegant black Grosser Mercedes Pullman limousines pulled up to slip eight, expelling a group of dignitaries. They gathered on the flag-draped platform beside the ship. After a short speech, an official introduced Mrs. Roosevelt. She stood amid a barrage of flashbulbs.

She was tall and slender. Her long, black coat sported a narrow fur collar. Her dark hat fitted close on her head, covering most of her hair. Her smile was pleasant, prominent front teeth gleaming as she swung the bottle of champagne with gusto.

I stood near enough to hear the crack of the smashing glass against the bow of the ship, to see white foam flowing down the hull, to hear the clapping and laughter that followed. The band played *The Stars and Stripes Forever* while the vessel slid down the way and into the waters of the west bank of the Hackensack River.

I felt exhilarated. I'd witnessed the show and seen Mrs. R. close and upfront.

After the workers drifted back to building ships, I stood a moment longer, watching as the guests moved towards their waiting limousines. I sighed. The launch had been a nice experience, but it was over. It was time to get back to my own work.

As I turned, I heard a high-pitched voice call out, "Oh dear, I forgot my purse. Just be a moment." I was close enough to hear the click of heels walking back along the deck just vacated.

That's Eleanor Roosevelt. I'd know that hat anywhere.

She was practically in front of me when I heard a faint scream and saw her disappear from my view. I bolted forward. She was in a hole, her upper arms resting on the wooden planks. The lower portion of her body was hidden beneath the wood deck, halfway through the platform where she had stood to launch the ship. She was struggling to pull herself up.

The sound of creaking wood alarmed me. I called, "Don't move, Mrs. Roosevelt. I'll help you."

She looked up. "Oh dear. Yes, please. Help me."

"Hold still," I said. "Don't wiggle."

I got down on my knees, placing my hands under her arms. As gently as I could, I attempted to lift the First Lady of the Land out of a hole.

It was going to take more than a quick lift. I stood with my feet spread and grabbed her just under the elbows. That worked better. Inch by inch, I freed her body to where she could sit on the edge of the broken wood. She was breathing heavily, but not as heavily as I was. I'd completed a mammoth feat. I'd lifted a woman nearly twice my size.

Between deep breaths, she said, "We did well, young lady. We did well, all thanks to you."

Zelda the Welder

"Happy to help, Mrs. Roosevelt," I panted.

Out of the corner of my eye, I saw her driver rush toward us. He was a large, burly man wearing a cap and jacket and a concerned look. He grasped the lady under her arms and set her on her feet. Amid her assurances that she was not hurt, that she could walk perfectly well, he carried her in his arms toward his waiting limousine.

She was not a heavily built woman but she was tall. My five-foot-two was no contest to her nearly six-foot. I bent to catch my breath. Then I spotted it. Her purse still lay where she had left it on the deck. I picked it up and ran to follow them. She had settled inside the limo, looking exhausted. I handed the purse to her, grinning at her look of astonishment.

Her answering smile was warm. "Oh, my. The silly cause of all the mischief. Thank you." She bent forward and grasped my hand. "What is your name, dear?"

"Zelda. Zelda Bea. I am so glad you're all right. I was afraid you might fall through before I could get to you."

"You saved me from a nasty incident, Zelda Bea. If you ever need anything,

anything at all, you have a friend here. I won't forget you." She looked straight into my eyes, her expression sincere. Patting my arm, she released me and settled into her seat.

I stepped back, giving a small wave. The excitement of the moment would be long remembered, although I might have to pinch myself to believe I hadn't dreamed it. The door of the black Mercedes closed, and they drove away.

To the departing limousine, I said, "I won't forget you either, Mrs. Roosevelt."

Behind me, I heard, "Me, neither." Big Joe stood there, a smirk searing his smarmy face. "Now we got that straight, how about getting back to work?"

"Yes, sir," I said. "But you had better treat me right, Mr. Morgan. You heard her. I'll call the White House if you don't." I couldn't believe my boldness. It must have been the afterglow of conversing with the President's wife. Right then, I didn't care what he thought. I plopped my shield down to hide a large grin as he walked away.

I had been welding for a short while when I thought I heard someone call my name. I glanced around.

Jimmy walked up. "Hey, did you miss me?"

"I'd rather ride than drive. Your car fixed?"

"Yup."

"Can you take the girls back home tonight? There's something I need to do."

"Sure. If you see them first, let them know I'll be waiting."

"Are you good for tomorrow?"

"You bet. I'll ferry you as usual."

"Great. See you then." I waved and returned to the job at hand.

CHAPTER TWENTY-ONE

At 4:10, I packed away my gear and left to gas up my car. The line was long as I pulled to the station. Good thing I'd started early. At 4:40, it was my turn at the pump. I showed the permit, and the attendant filled my tank.

Pulling out, I spotted Mary standing at the entrance. She waved, and I stopped, rolling down my window. "What happened? Didn't you find Jimmy?"

"I decided to go home with you. You're up to something, and I want to know what."

I stared at her. Cars behind me honked. "Get in." I cocked my head. "Where's Annie?"

"With Jimmy. She has to get home."

"And you don't?"

She gave a little smile. "I'd rather go with you."

"Okay. But if you gum up my plans, I'll throw you out of the car, wherever we are." I grinned at her to show her I really wouldn't do that.

In the parking lot, I pulled into my previous space—across and three cars away from Big Joe's Lincoln. The yard had begun to empty out, other cars pulling into vacated spaces, but Big Joe's car was still there. *Thank you, God.*

I did a lot of God thanking these days. Guess I needed all the help I could get. After I parked, I jumped out of the car, got my large-brimmed felt hat out of the trunk, then hopped in beside Mary again. "Okay, so here's the plan. We're going to follow Big Joe home, but he mustn't know."

"And why do you want to do that? I thought you hated the guy."

I turned to face her, forcing her look at me. "Mary, the way he acts, he wants me to think he knows where Janice is. He talks like he does. He says she's on vacation in Miami."

"Miami? Why Miami?"

"I don't know. Maybe because there's snow on the ground in New Jersey. The point is, he's boldface lying. He's sweet on her. Did you know that?"

Mary looked confused. "He is?"

"Anyway, I want to see where he lives. She could be there, you know. Against her will."

"Oh God, Zelda. And you're planning to rescue her?" She thumped her forehead with her hand. "You know what, that's crazy. Really crazy. What movie was that in?"

"Listen, girlfriend, if you knew him like I do, you wouldn't trust him either. It's called female intuition, okay? And I don't know what else I can do. Anyway, if you want to stay with me, you'll keep low and hush up. I don't want you to get hurt."

Mary's eyebrows rose, her eyes wide as she studied me—like she'd met me for the first time. "Okay," she said, "You're the boss," and slunk down to the floor on the passenger side. "Will this do?"

I didn't feel jovial, but she made me laugh. I forced myself to relax. "I only want you to be safe. Okay?"

She looked sheepish. "I only want to help."

A half smile on my face, I took my eyes from her to scrutinize the lot. "I know. And I'm glad you're here. I didn't like being alone on this."

"Well, you're always there for me."

Then I spotted him walking leisurely toward his car. "Get down," I ordered in a loud whisper.

She scrunched beside me and squeaked, "Oh, dear."

I hadn't taken the time to remove the bandanna I wore to keep my hair out of the way while I worked. I pulled it off now, letting my hair fall loose to my shoulders. I put on the felt hat, adjusting the large brim so it covered a good half of my face. I thought of sunglasses, but decided they would be too obvious. I threw a woolen scarf over my shoulders and knotted it, covering my chin.

"What are we going to do when we get there?" Mary asked. Her voice was subdued, drifting up from the floor where she sat.

"I haven't thought that far ahead yet."

More cars drove off, being replaced with the night-crew. Unlike the daytime, the lot was half empty. Big Joe seemed in no hurry, stopping several times to look around the vast lot. Finally, he reached his car.

He stopped to light a cigarette, then turned in my direction for what seemed a long moment. My mouth went dry, and my hands tightened around the steering wheel. Joe blew out smoke while he stared. He shook his head, shrugged, and took another drag. Leaning against the car, he finished his cigarette and flicked the butt away. Finally, he got in. Starting the motor, he slowly pulled his car out and onto the highway.

CHAPTER TWENTY-TWO

We were heading northeast toward New York City. Snow lay melted on the roads in a slushy, slippery mess. I didn't like driving under these conditions, although the 35 mph wartime speed limit created less splashing. Most cars were traveling no more than 25 mph this evening.

Mary chatted nonstop beside me, mostly to herself as I wasn't paying a bit of attention. I grasped the steering wheel in both hands, jaw clenched as I stared out the windshield at the congestion of slow moving vehicles. I never paid attention to the traffic when Jimmy drove.

Big Joe's Lincoln remained six cars in front of us. I wanted to keep it that way. I had worked at staying at least seventy-five feet behind since he pulled away from the Federal parking lot and turned left down main highway US 1.

The ride stretched ahead, a mass of intersections and turnoffs. We drove over the Queensboro Bridge and crossed the East River, leaving New York City behind. We were in Queens, traveling east on Jericho Turnpike. Where the devil was he going? I knew he lived in New Jersey, only minutes from Federal. I had gotten his location from Miss Stern, Mr. Hansen's secretary. While she wouldn't give me the exact address, she did tell me his whereabouts. So where was he going?

It was another fifteen minutes before Big Joe pulled off the highway and turned onto a narrow road. Other cars made the turn. I was still concealed behind them.

We traveled north a short distance and turned right, passing through Little Neck and on to Great Neck. We were in an undeveloped, woodsy area. The cars in front of me turned off, spiraling away to smaller roads.

We left the concrete to ride on blacktop. We were on the northern fork of Long Island on a road called Rabbit Run. We had left Queens County a while back and were in Nassau County. Through the trees, I saw the Long Island Sound. The large body of water traveled Long Island's northern coastline to the Atlantic Ocean.

Zelda the Welder

It was seven o'clock in the evening. The area was quiet. Only Big Joe's car and mine remained on the road. It had been dusk when we left Jersey, and now it was full nighttime. Lighted windows shone in the few houses we passed. There were no streetlights.

I slowed, dropping back, trying to be inconspicuous. If Mary hadn't been with me, I would have lost my nerve and turned around, gone back to Maspeth—we weren't that far away. She kept my spirits up, joking about Big Joe and how he would feel if he knew we were on his tail. That's how she put it. On his tail, giggling every time she said it. I didn't have the heart to tell her I thought he probably already knew. How could he not?

I worried that he was deliberately leading us into the woods.

CHAPTER TWENTY-THREE

When the telephone rang, Ida glanced at the grandfather clock in the hall. It was nearly 7:30. Unusual for anyone to call her, she thought, especially this late. It must be Zelda. She gripped the armrests of her chair and pushed up from her post by the radio.

"Hello?" she whispered into the mouthpiece, trying not to disturb Billy. His ear was practically against the speaker as he listened to *The Lone Ranger*.

"Is this Ida?" she heard from the phone's earpiece.

"It is."

"This is Sadie Silver, Zelda's friend. Zelda isn't answering her telephone. She left both your numbers at the nurses' desk—in case."

"She *is* late tonight. She drove her car to work today. I haven't heard from her, but she should be home soon."

"I wanted her to know I'm leaving the hospital tomorrow morning. Can you tell her, please? I don't want her to wonder where I am."

"How are you getting home?"

"By cab. Zelda will have to bring Billy to me."

"Billy. Ah, yes. I'm glad to get this chance to speak to you, Sadie. We all love your Billy. I was hoping I could come and visit you both once he leaves here."

"That would be nice. I'm sure Billy would be pleased to see a friend. Any chance I could say hello to him now?"

"Hold on. I'll pry him away from his show." She raised her voice. "Billy, I have someone on the phone who wants to talk to you."

All scrubbed and pajama clad, Billy was in his usual position—on his belly beside the radio, knees bent, chubby little feet in the air behind him. He glanced up with a serious expression on his rosy-cheeked face. "Mommy?"

"No, sweetie. It's your grandmother. She wants to say hello to you."

"Okay." Billy rose and ran to the phone. "Hi, Gram. You coming home?"

"Yes, I am, Billy. Tomorrow. Are you being a good boy?"

"Yes. We had maca—maca…" He looked up at Ida.

"Macaroni and cheese," Ida said into the mouthpiece, laughing.

"Is Mommy working?" Billy asked. "I want Mommy. Is she coming home?"

"Not yet, Billy. We'll both see her soon, though. Just be good and make her proud of you. I know you do."

"Okay. Bye, Gram." He handed the receiver to Ida, who replaced it on its curved metal hook. With his blue eyes large and pensive, he asked, "Where's Aunt Zelda?"

"Just delayed at work, sweet boy. She'll be home any minute."

"Okay." He smiled and ran back to the radio. It wouldn't do to miss any of the excitement there.

Except for an occasional house, all I saw was wild virgin woods—tall pines, low bushes. I was wondering just how far Big Joe was going when he slowed his car and made a left turn, parking in a small clearing.

I continued driving down the road, heart pounding.

"Don't you think we should turn around now? Go home?" Mary said.

"Write down that address. Maybe there is a reason he came all this way." I had no idea what I was suggesting until I said it. "Could Janice be in that house?"

Mary looked at me like I had lost my mind. "Why would he bring her so far? Why bring her anywhere? Zelda, the whole idea is stupid."

"I know. You're right."

The country road was narrow. I spotted an opening in the brush to turn around and edged into a space between some tall oak trees. Winter-brown leaves hung from its branches.

I shut off the motor. Frustrated, I lay my forehead against the steering wheel. The brim of my hat struck it and pushed back from my brow. Closing my eyes, I rested that way for several moments, my mind throbbing with more questions.

Mary glanced at the small gold watch on her wrist. "It's getting late. How long are we going to hang around? There is nothing more we can do here."

"Why did he drive all the way to Long Island?" I murmured thoughtfully.

"Why so far for nothing? Do you think he knew we were following?"

Mary shrugged. "It was your idea."

"This *would* be a great place to hide someone," I said. "What if Janice *is* inside? What if he brought her here? How can we just leave? Do you think we could get into that house?"

Mary gaped at me, eyes wide. "I have a better question. Which would you prefer? Would you rather get us killed or arrested for trespassing?"

I ignored her. "Am I a complete fool for believing he would abduct Janice and bring her here?"

"What do you want?" Mary asked. "You won't take my advice, so what do we do now? Do we break down the door? Call the police? I'm here for you, only make some sense."

"We could come back tomorrow. He'll be gone then." I swallowed the panic welling up inside me and reached into my pocket to touch the bit of silk. "I can't just forget the whole thing."

Mary gasped. She put her hand on my arm and turned to glance behind us. Her face blanched. "Zelda, honey, I think we'd better get out of here. Right this minute. Oh, please hurry."

The crunch of footsteps upon icy snow reached me. I glanced around. The moon lit up the stand of oak to almost daylight, casting long shadows on the area where my car was parked. The tramp of footsteps grew louder.

"Get down, Mary," I hissed as a man walked out of the trees and came directly toward us. I saw him clearly, and my throat tightened. I could barely breathe. Oh, no. He's going to catch us. Damn, damn, damn.

With shaking hands, I reached for the ignition and turned the key. The motor turned over. Big Joe Morgan was about ten feet away when my Oldsmobile leapt to life with a blast from the tailpipe. The wheels jumped, and the car jerked forward.

Twisting in my seat, I looked through the back window, cursing the large brim of my hat that flopped across my face and over my eyes. I gunned the engine, tires spinning as I backed out of our hiding place. Big Joe jumped aside. I skidded and swerved, barely missing him. Turning the steering wheel sharply, I swung the car around and headed down the small road the way we came. I urged my car to go faster. We sped down the country road toward Rabbit Run.

"He knew we were there," Mary said.

"He knew he was being followed. I don't think he knew *who* was following. If we're lucky, he didn't recognize us."

Mary glared at me. "He could have gotten your license plate number."

"I don't think I gave him a chance. I almost hit him."

Mary slumped in her seat. "We should find out who lives in that house."

I didn't answer. I concentrated on driving. The streets were empty. Most of suburbia was at dinner or had their ears close to the radio listening to the latest news on the war. My tires squealed as we left the blacktop and pulled onto concrete. We were again on Jericho Turnpike. My speedometer read forty-five, fifty.

"Hey," Mary screamed. "What are you doing? You want to kill us?"

"Sorry." I slowed to thirty-five. "I was afraid he'd come after us."

We turned off the Turnpike to travel west on Queens Boulevard. Once at Grand

Avenue, I made a left. My watch read eight o'clock when I finally turned onto Sixty-Third Street.

I was home, somewhat the worse for wear, trembling from fatigue and fright, but still functioning. In the darkness, my street resembled a long, somber tunnel flanked by narrow, two story houses. Streetlights glowed like cloud-wrapped stars in the chill night air. The only other light came from an occasional window.

The city's plows had pushed the accumulated snow to the side of the road. It lay at the edges of the sidewalk in piles three feet high. The light from the street lamps hit the gray-white, frozen tops, making them glitter like stars. A gust of wind whistled by, breaking the quiet of the street as my car came to a stop in front of my house.

"It's late," I told Mary. "I'll make us some supper before I take you home."

Mary hadn't said much all the way to my house. Now she turned to me. "I was thinking about Janice, perhaps alone somewhere, perhaps frightened."

I shut off the motor, clinging to the steering wheel with both hands until I calmed my racing heart. "I'm not much help, am I? I was unable to confront the man I believe abducted my friend. I lost my nerve. I ran scared, perhaps did more harm than good."

"Well, I'm glad you did—run that is. Big Joe is not someone to cross." Mary took my hand in hers. "Listen, honey, we will find Janice. But we'll do it the right way. We'll call that detective friend of yours. What was his name?"

"John O'Reilly's not my friend. He's the police." I paused, then reached into my denim pocket, taking out the small piece of leopard-print silk. I held it for Mary to see. "I found this today."

Mary looked puzzled. "What is it?"

"A piece of scarf."

Mary's face showed recognition. "It's torn."

"It tore as I pulled it out of Big Joe Morgan's closed car trunk. It's *her* scarf. Our Janice's scarf."

"Okay. So what are you saying?"

"Rusty saw him bringing a duffle bag to his car the day Janice went missing. What if she was in that bag? What if her scarf got caught in the trunk when he was lifting her out after he shoved her in?"

"And what if he just found her scarf and kept it?" Mary asked.

"She loved that scarf. It wouldn't be just lying around. Mary, he has to know where she is."

She didn't answer.

I shivered and fumbled with my door handle. "Billy's at Ida's. Since Janice's mother is in the hospital, Ida minds him while I'm at work. It's been good for her, takes her out of her doldrums. She misses her own son dreadfully. Babysitting Billy was a gift."

Mary nodded, her expression compassionate. "Is that her there?"

Across the street, Ida's front door opened. Ida stood silhouetted in the brightness for a moment before coming out and closing the door behind her. Waving, she stepped down from her stoop and hurried across the road toward my car. The wind whipped her red quilt robe behind her.

"You're finally home," she called, her voice reaching us before she did. Her smile was broad. "Billy's been asleep for half an hour. I tucked him into Peter's bed. He's sleeping so soundly, I wouldn't want to disturb him."

"I wouldn't think of disturbing little Billy. I'm so sorry I'm late, Ida. We had an unexpected evening. This is Mary. She works at Federal with me."

"Hello, Ida," Mary said.

"Have you two eaten yet? I have leftovers." Ida's breath floated on the frosty night air like a soft mist.

"That's kind of you, but I can make something simple for Mary and me." I took her cold hand. "Thank you, Ida. I couldn't handle all this without you."

"One more thing. Sadie phoned. She's leaving the hospital tomorrow. She'll be getting a cab, but Billy has to be brought home. I'd be happy to volunteer, if it's all right with you."

"It would be a big help if you could take him home for me."

"That's what I hoped. Good, then it is settled."

I sighed. I would miss the little guy, and Ida would be devastated without him. But I had things to do tomorrow. I had to tell Detective O'Reilly about the scarf, about what happened tonight, about the house in Great Neck. And I still hadn't told him about the purse. I felt time closing in on me.

I couldn't do anything more tonight. And I would fall over if I didn't have some food soon. I opened my car door and felt a cold blast of wind. "Ida, you'll catch your death. You're not dressed for this weather. I'll stop by in the morning to say goodbye to Billy."

The wind picked up and Ida wrapped her robe more tightly around herself. "Enjoy your supper. Nice meeting you, Mary."

"Bye, Ida," Mary called as she stepped from the car.

We climbed over the snow bank and walked to the house. I unlocked my door. Warm air and the plaintive cry of Meow greeted us.

"Poor baby, you're hungry too. I'm so sorry." I bent down and ruffled his fur.

I ushered Mary inside. This was the first time she'd visited my home. As I hung our coats in the hall closet, I said, "Listen. Why don't you stay with me tonight? It would be silly to drive you home this late. You can have Billy's bed."

"Thanks. I'm bushed."

"Good. Follow me," I said, heading for my small kitchen. "There's the bathroom if you want to wash up. Then have a seat and you'll see what I can make in no time at all." I opened my icebox. "I have some chopped meat and salad fixings. I had planned to make dinner tonight for Billy and Ida. I hadn't expected today to be such a catastrophe."

Mary pulled out a chair, but didn't sit. "Let me help."

"How about you set the table while I boil some water?"

"Just point to where everything is."

I pointed, then got out my large spaghetti pot and shook some salt into the water. When it boiled, I put in half a package of thin spaghetti. While waiting, I pulled out my favorite cookbook and located my marker indicating the pages for spaghetti sauces.

"What have you got there?" Mary asked.

I held it up. "*The Joy of Cooking*, by Irma Rombauer. When I'm hungry, I invariably crave pasta. Tonight it will be Quick Meat Sauce, ala Irma and Zelda. I have made all of the eighteen spaghetti sauces."

"I have that book. It's famous. I only made about three things from it, but it was fun." Mary shrugged. "What else can I do?"

"Check the cupboard," I called over my shoulder.

"Ha!" Mary's grin was wide as she took out a bottle of Chianti. It sported a red bow. "Obviously a gift leftover from some holiday past." She placed it on the counter then took down the wine glasses. "Now what?"

"How are you at making a salad?"

"Only the best."

"Swell. I have the fixings in the icebox." I took oil and vinegar from an upper cabinet and put it by the sink. I reached for the salad bowl and my favorite chopping knife and handed them to Mary, along with a white apron with dancing pink cherubs.

"Get to work," I ordered.

She rolled up her sleeves. "Eating feeds the body. Cooking feeds the soul."

After everything that had happened, we *were* having fun. Cooking always helped me clear my head, and tonight, with Mary helping, it was a treat.

"We make a great team," I said. "I'm so glad you dumped yourself on me."

Mary grinned and sprinkled me with water as she washed the vegetables and greens at the sink.

I left her to the salad and turned back to my boiling water. The spaghetti was cooking nicely. Into the quarter cup of olive oil I had warming in a frying pan, I put two minced cloves of garlic and a quarter cup of chopped onion. When they were properly softened, I added small chunks of the chopped beef and pork, stirring it slowly to blend and cook evenly. In my saucepot, I emptied one large can of tomato sauce and one small can of tomato paste, stirring as it heated, then added the meat and onions and garlic to the sauce. I sprinkled in salt and pepper, oregano, parsley, and paprika, and let the whole of it slowly simmer until we were ready for it. This was my Quick Meat Sauce, and every bit as good as the five hour version.

It was time to drain the pasta and place it into a bowl, add two tablespoons of butter and stir until melted, then introduce a little sauce to the mix. The rest of the meat sauce would sit on the stove over a low flame while we ate Mary's perfect salad.

Through a mouthful of crispy greens, I said, "I'm going to skip work in the morning and ask Detective O'Reilly to come over. How about sticking around? He might want your take on that business at the house in Great Neck."

"You think he'll take us seriously?"

I took a sip of wine, felt its warmth flow down my throat. "I think he will. He's listened to me before."

"I do want to find out what today was all about. Let's just hope Big Joe didn't recognize us." Mary wiped her lips with her napkin. "You know, this is the best meal I've ever eaten."

I laughed. "That is because we were really hungry."

It was ten o'clock before we finished washing the dishes, and we were yawning after each sentence.

"Let's get some sleep," I told her. "Tomorrow we'll call Jimmy and tell him not to pick us up, tell Federal we'll be late. We'll call Detective O'Reilly and talk him into taking us to the Great Neck house."

That was the plan.

CHAPTER TWENTY-FOUR

After I showed Mary her sleeping quarters, I changed the sheets and pillowcase on the bed Billy used. "Sleep well. If you need anything—"

"This is fine," she said. "I'm so tired I'll be out before you make it to your room."

I wished I could have said the same. I tossed and turned and slept fitfully, having all sorts of weird dreams. In one, I was chased by a huge bull wearing a white cowboy hat and shiny black boots. Its face looked like Big Joe's, but it had horns curling through the hat. Its bullhorn moo was so loud it woke up all of Long Island, and everyone crowded into the streets yelling, *not in my house, not in my house. No one's home in my house.*

After twisting and sighing most of the night, I finally dropped off for an hour before the alarm went off. Today I didn't need any help from Meow. I hopped out of bed, ready to challenge Mr. Bull Morgan again. Bull Morgan. Wow, I'd hate to slip with that one in his presence—although the name did sound every bit as appropriate as Big Joe.

First, I phoned Jimmy, telling him not to stop for Mary or me today. Then I called Ida and asked her to bring Billy and come for breakfast. We could make it a fun goodbye.

I called the shipyard and told them Mary and I would be out today, claiming an emergency. I would think of what kind later. I went into Mary's room. She was still deep in sleep.

Quietly, I packed Billy's clothes and set out a fresh shirt and pants for him to wear home to Sadie. When I was finished, I put all his things into the wagon and rolled it into the living room.

Then I went to the kitchen to plan breakfast. I had enough eggs and milk to make pancakes. Everyone loved them, and it could be kind of festive. I thumbed through *The Joy of Cooking.* There were seventeen recipes for pancakes. I chuckled thinking Crepes Suzette would be festive if I had an hour to make them and had all the special ingredients. They looked detailed and alarmingly complicated, and not good for a little boy. I settled for the everyday kind, made with milk and butter and flour, as Irma instructed.

Pancakes were simple, so I decided to call O'Reilly before I cooked. If he wasn't in yet, I'd leave a message for him to call me back. I had just reached for the phone when it rang, startling me. I jumped, dropping the receiver, and fumbled to pick it up.

"Sorry," I mumbled.

"Miss Bea?"

"Yes, this is Zelda Bea."

"Detective O'Reilly here."

My imagination ran wild. *Janice. She was found. She was dead? She was alive but hurt?* "Yes, Detective O'Reilly. What have you learned?"

"I thought you would want to know I received a message from Janice Bates."

"A message?"

"Yes, from Miss Bates. She said she wanted the search for her to stop. She apologized because you were annoying the police in the first place. She said you were an alarmist and to pay you no mind, or something like that. I'm trying to read the sergeant's illegible handwriting."

"Excuse me, Detective, but when did she leave the message?"

"I thought I told you. Last night. Around eleven-thirty."

"It wasn't Janice, Detective. As a matter of fact, I was going to call you myself with some additional information."

"Hold on." There was a long pause. I was ready to hang up when he finally came back on the line. "The Sergeant on duty took the call. He's here now. He says, yes, it was a woman. She gave her name as Janice Bates."

"Detective, you must know Janice's history. She has a small son she adores and a mother who cares for him when she is at work. She wouldn't go away without letting them know first. The person who spoke to your sergeant is an impostor. The fact that they would take the time to do so has me even more concerned. Whoever phoned must be getting nervous. They are trying to throw you off their track. Janice could be in further danger. Is it possible we could meet at my home this morning? I have something to show you. I would go to the station, but the place I want to take you is on Long Island."

I could almost hear O'Reilly thinking *that dumb dame, what's up her craw now?* I felt my face turn hot.

"I'll be there as soon as I can. And you better know what you're talking about. If this is a wild goose chase, I could lock you up. My time is valuable, you know."

I heard a chuckle, and then a click as he put the receiver back on its hook.

"It isn't funny," I said to an empty line, hanging the receiver up with a bang.

Mary stood in the doorway, listening. She stepped into the room. "So, is your detective coming?"

"He said he'd be here. We better be ready. I have to make pancakes for Ida and Billy and us. And I have to get dressed. Let's move, friend." I rushed to the kitchen and pulled out the frying pan.

"Hold it," Mary said. "You get dressed, and I'll start things. Don't worry, I know my way around a kitchen. Go. Scoot."

The doorbell rang, and Billy's high-pitched voice tumbled ahead of him into the room. He ran into my outstretched arms. "Gram is coming home. Aunt Ida is taking me." His grin was as wide as his chubby cheeks would allow. His eyes sparkled like the most wonderful thing in the whole world was happening. "Mommy, too?" he asked, his curls bouncing as he nodded his head.

CHAPTER TWENTY-FIVE

Between Irma Rombauer, Mary, and me, breakfast was a huge success.

When Billy and Ida were ready to leave, I kissed Billy goodbye six times, promising I'd see him soon. I told Ida, for the fourth time, "Please, let me know how everything goes at Sadie's."

Together, Mary and I straightened up the kitchen. I wiped the smooth, red enamel top on my kitchen table. I had opened both extensions to make room for all of us. Now I slid them underneath. Mary put the shining silverware in the drawer. That done, the kitchen spotless, we sat down to wait for John O'Reilly to arrive.

"What do we do if your policeman doesn't agree to go with us to the Great Neck house?" Mary asked.

"He's not a *policeman*, and he's not *mine*, and I won't drag you along if you would rather not go, but I intend to see the inside of that house today. With or without O'Reilly. I'd rather do it the right way, but one way or another I'm getting in there while Joe Morgan is at work."

"I'll stay with you. I can't let you go alone."

"Thanks."

We listened to the radio while we waited for O'Reilly to arrive. I told Mary about the new indoor shipyard that was opening in an old warehouse. I kept glancing at the clock, getting more anxious as the time passed. When I heard him pull up, I ran to the front window. I watched him get out of his car, close the door, and glance up and down the street before venturing to my home. Nothing like surveying the territory, I thought, opening the front door before he could ring.

"Hello, Detective O'Reilly. Please come in."

He stepped inside, taking off his hat.

In the living room, Mary looked up from the morning paper and smiled.

I read her look. *He's cute*. I rolled my eyes, then turned to the detective. "This is my friend, Mary Colman. She works at Federal, too."

O'Reilly nodded. "Miss Colman." Then he turned his attention back to me.

"Shall we get right to the point? We have not been able to find anything more on your friend's whereabouts. She was listed as a missing person until this morning. When we received the phone call from her, we took her off the list. What is it you have to show me to debunk that? I hope it justifies a two-hour drive."

Mary covered her mouth, hiding a grin. If I couldn't even get *her* to take me seriously, what hope did I have?

I took a breath to steady my nerve. Everything hinged on whether or not I could convince him. I opened the trinket box on the end table. "I found this. It's Janice's purse. I bought it for her birthday."

Mary stood, suddenly solemn. "You didn't tell me you found that."

"Where?" The detective turned it over in his hands.

"In the shed on top of the DE."

"Where you found the blood?"

"Yes."

Mary caught my eye. She mouthed the word *blood*.

"So, she dropped her purse," he said.

"She didn't just drop it, Detective. If you drop something, you go back and pick it up. This has her identification. It has forty-two dollars. You don't just drop it and walk away." I straightened my shoulders. "But more than that, it proves she was there. On top of the DE that morning. I think she went into the shed looking for me, and she saw someone doing something they ought not be doing. Probably Joe Morgan."

O'Reilly listened, not saying anything until I stopped talking. He had a stern look and spoke like he was questioning a child. "Do you really believe Joe Morgan is capable of kidnapping?"

"He acts suspicious—the things he says, the way he acts. He became enraged when my scarf fluttered in his face, saying Janice tried that, too. Who gets angry at something like that? But here, let me show you what else I found." I reached into my pocket and brought out the small piece of leopard silk. It didn't look very impressive in my hand. "This belonged to Janice. I found it hanging out of Big Joe's trunk. I pulled it, and it tore."

"And you think it belongs to Miss Bates?"

"I was with Janice when she bought it. I wanted it, too, and there was only one of this print, so we haggled over it." I brought the slip of fabric to his nose. "Here. Smell it. That's her perfume. I would know Channel N° 5 anywhere."

He put on his hat. "Look, Miss Bea—"

"I'm not making this up, Detective. It's her scarf. We laughed every time she wore it. I called her the leopard lady."

"So you base all your supposition on a bit of cloth sticking out of his trunk?" He reached for the remnant, turning it over and over. There wasn't anything soiling the fabric—no blood, no stains—just a torn piece of silk. He handed it back to me.

I closed my eyes, steeling myself. Time for my big finish. "Last night, after work, Mary and I followed Big Joe out of Federal. I hoped he would lead us to where he put Janice. He took us to a house in the woods near Great Neck."

"Long Island," he said.

I nodded. "He parked in the yard. We drove past then pulled into some trees. I was trying to think of a way to get into the house. All of a sudden, he came rushing at us out of the trees. I didn't know what he'd do. I spun the car around and sped home."

He took out his yellow notebook. "What time was this?"

"Around seven. Right, Mary?"

"Did you get an address?"

"We wanted to," Mary said, "but it was too dark. And spooky."

"Let me get this straight," O'Reilly said. "The two of you followed the foreman from New Jersey to Long Island. He stopped at a house. His home? Someone else's home? And then you drove off."

He made it sound like the silly ranting of two stupid girls.

I quelled an impulse to stamp my foot. "Detective O'Reilly, when he came out of the woods towards us, I panicked and sped away. I shouldn't have. What if he has Janice locked up in that house?"

"We can take you there," Mary said.

"So, what do you want me to do? Go to the house with you? Break in?"

"It does sound wild when *you* say it, but yes, that *is* what I want. Janice would never go with him unless forced. And she didn't make that phone call."

"Two things, Miss Bea," O'Reilly said. "Long Island is out of my jurisdiction. And even if it weren't, I would need a search warrant to break into someone's house. If I could even get one on such a flimsy a reason as you've given me."

"How else are we going to find out? What if she's there? Big Joe was obviously upset at being followed. I tried not to be seen, but it isn't easy following someone from New Jersey to the backwoods of Long Island's North Shore without being noticed. He spotted the car. We just hope he didn't recognize us."

Mary put her arm around me. "He's hiding something, Detective."

"Do you truly believe so? Or has Miss Bea convinced you it is so?"

Mary smiled. "I guess you had to be there. I was. If he didn't abduct her, I'd bet he knows a lot more than he's saying."

The detective turned thoughtfully, hat in hand, and strolled to the window. "If what you say is true, a young woman could be hurt or even dead. You have given me only circumstantial evidence, Miss Bea, but it has some merit." He stared out of the window and continued speaking as if to himself. "Perhaps the Great Neck police department would like to come with me to check out this house."

I waited, wringing the bit of silk in my hands.

He turned, a resigned smile on his face. "All right. This is what we will do. I'll drive up there with you. We'll check out the place from the *outside*, find out who lives there. If it is Morgan's we'll see what we can do from there." He stared me down. "We will not go into that house, any house, without a search warrant. Have you got that?"

CHAPTER TWENTY-SIX

I let out a sigh, then smiled. "Thank you, Detective. I was afraid you wouldn't want to go." I walked to the closet and withdrew our coats. "Come on, Mary."

O'Reilly stopped, blocking my way to the door. "Just a minute, Miss Bea. I said you could go with me to see the house. I didn't say we'd make it a party."

"Mary was with me yesterday. She cares as much as I do."

Mary took her coat and hugged it. She pouted just enough to look her sweet, beguiling best. "Detective, I can't let Janice down. And I promised Zelda I'd stick with her all the way."

Which was a bit of a lie right there, but close enough for Good Girl points. I did feel better having her with me.

O'Reilly's eyes, lids at half-mast, lingered a few seconds on Mary. He turned to me, about to say something, then back to Mary. He sighed. "Okay. Let's go." He started for the door, then stopped and turned, nearly causing the three of us to collide. "One condition." His eyes swept from me to Mary and back. "You don't do anything but sit in the car while I take a look around. Nobody gets out. Nobody goes into the house. Nobody does anything. Understood?"

Unblinking, Mary nodded. I just buttoned my coat.

"All right," he said, "but remember, we aren't even sure it *is* Morgan's house. After I see the area, I'll have to stop at the local police station. Perhaps they will know more about the place."

We walked outside and took our seats in O'Reilly's shining, 1943 Ford Sedan, tire walls gleaming whiter than the snow piled at the side of the road. I sat up front. Mary sat in back. It was quiet in the car.

Great Neck wasn't far, and at ten-thirty in the morning the roads were fairly empty. I directed O'Reilly, and in twenty-five minutes we were back on Rabbit Run in the pine forest I'd fled.

Using the stand of oak trees as my landmark, I found the house. It was surrounded by a picket fence that leaned precariously. The night before, all I had seen was a roof and a driveway. Today, in bright daylight, the house appeared smaller than I had thought. The shingle siding had once been white. Now much of it was mousey-grey, worn down to bare wood. What windows I could see were boarded up. Did *anyone* live here?

I glanced at winter-dormant rosebushes spreading leafless branches in what must have once been a lovely garden. I could imagine a well-tended lawn beneath what was now a large, white, icy blanket. Edging the narrow driveway leading to the porch were evergreen privet hedges laden with heavy snow. It snowed a lot more on Long Island than in New Jersey.

There was only one set of tire tracks, frozen now, pulling in and backing out. My guess was they were there from yesterday. Big Joe's Lincoln. One set of footprints showed in front and continued around the side of the building. From my window, I couldn't see more than half way to the back.

O'Reilly threw us a glance that read, *stay*. He opened his door and stepped into the snow, adding his footprints as he walked. He had just reached the front steps when a large, shaggy collie came bounding around the corner, barking loudly. O'Reilly stopped in his tracks, not moving a muscle.

From the backseat, I heard Mary gasp. I held my breath and watched.

His back to us, O'Reilly squatted while reaching into his jacket pocket. He held out one hand while he patted the gold and white dog on the head with the other. I could barely hear his voice, couldn't make out his words. The barking stopped, and the dog wagged a lush tail, looking at him like it had found a friend. O'Reilly walked up the icy steps, the dog following.

I smiled. *Some watchdog.*

The detective knocked on the front door. When no one answered, he carefully stepped around the porch past a stand of white birch growing on one side of the property. He turned the corner, making his way toward the back. Both he and the collie disappeared from sight.

Mary said, "I can't imagine anyone living here."

"I know. It looks abandoned." From where I sat, the place had a falling-apart look. I noted a drooping gutter filled with snow, ready to fall to the ground.

O'Reilly came back into view. He stopped several times to peer between the cracks of the boarded windows. He pushed aside a board here and there, the better to see inside. After about ten minutes of that, he strode to a tilting mailbox at roadside. He didn't touch it, just looked, jotting something down in the small, yellow book he carried in his inside pocket.

Whispering to the collie, O'Reilly once more slipped his hand into his pocket, bringing a treat to the dog, who nuzzled it, turned, and trotted back the way it had come. The detective watched a moment, then got into the car. He reached into his glove compartment and took out a book of maps. Thumbing through them, he found what he was looking for, then closed the book with a snap.

"The Great Neck police station is next," O'Reilly said, in his usual taciturn manner. He backed his car out of the driveway, leaving another set of tracks in the snow.

If Big Joe returns, he'll know someone was here.

Great Neck was a charming, tidy town. The older buildings lent a nostalgic aura. It was now close to noon, and the main street bustled with the lunch crowd. As we drove past, I noticed the stores were crowded with well-dressed shoppers. They could have cleaned out a zoo for the fur coats I saw, all styles and types and colors. No doubt the people of Great Neck were wealthy.

Suddenly, Mary tapped me on the shoulder. Bouncing up and down, she squealed, "Look. Look over there. Fanny Brice just went into that dress shop."

I twisted in my seat to look, but I was too late to see anyone entering the store. "You sure?"

"It *was her*. I read about this town in *House and Gardens*. Lots of celebrities live here. There are a whole slew of them. I remember a few names in the article. Eugene O'Neill, he of the great Broadway plays. And some of those funny people—Groucho Marx, W. C. Fields, Sid Caesar. And they *did* mention Fanny Brice. I know it was her I saw. Wow. I guess it's the proximity to Broadway that draws them. They sure have a pretty little town."

"Yes," I said. "It's lovely."

"Do you think we'll ever live like them? I mean, all those expensive houses and everything?"

I shrugged. "Perhaps someday after the war, when all our boys are home and we can pick up our lives again, we can think about fancy homes. All I can think about now is finding Janice alive and well."

Mary was in another world. "Just the same, someday I shall write a book and be famous, and then I'll move here, or somewhere as exquisite."

"That's nice." I gazed out the window at the people walking about and entering stores. "It looks like the war hasn't slowed the town down much. Shoppers are spending money like they were printing it themselves."

What was Big Joe doing here? He wasn't rich or famous. Why was there one ramshackle house amid all this opulence? Did Joe know the owner? Or had he pulled in there at random so he could find out who was following him? It nagged at me. I had to learn the truth.

I glanced across at O'Reilly, his eyes straight ahead, hands firmly on the steering wheel. We had driven through the town's main street and hadn't located the police station yet. I spotted a uniformed cop, his nightstick rhythmically thumping against his pant leg as he walked. I rolled down the window. "Sir?"

The officer sauntered toward the car. "Yes, ma'am?"

O'Reilly pulled to the curb and stopped.

"Can you direct us to the nearest police station?" I said.

The officer bent and looked in at O'Reilly, speaking over my head as if I didn't matter. "Sir? Are you looking for the station?"

O'Reilly's face darkened. He went for his wallet and showed his badge. "I'm Detective John O'Reilly from Kearny, New Jersey. I have business at your precinct."

"Certainly, Detective." With a polite smile, the officer directed us down two more blocks and over one, pointing with his nightstick.

I waved goodbye cheerily as we continued on our way.

O'Reilly took his eyes off the road to glare at me. "Just so you know, I was getting there with no problem, Miss Bea. Next time, you will ask me before you ask for directions."

I lowered my head, mumbling, "Sorry."

Mary gave a soft snort from the backseat.

It didn't take long to reach the stationhouse. The long, redbrick building spread its two stories across a large lawn. Several police cars were parked on the shoveled blacktop. O'Reilly pulled his Ford into an empty spot close to the front of the building, his law enforcement placard in his front window.

He beckoned for Mary and me to join him. Double glass doors led us inside. The area bustled with uniformed policemen entering and leaving. At the usual raised desk, a heavy-set police sergeant was on the phone. His beefy hand wrapped around the tall candlestick base as he spoke into the mouthpiece. Half a dead cigarette jumped with each word as it dangled from his lips.

We waited while he finished his conversation. After about two minutes of nodding and mumbling, he replaced the earpiece on its holder and turned solemn eyes to us. "Yes?"

O'Reilly showed his badge. "I'm Detective John O'Reilly, Kearny precinct."

"How can I help you, Detective?"

"I'm following a lead on a missing person report. What I found led me to your town and an empty house. From the outside it looks abandoned. Sealed up. We need to locate the owner. Any help there?"

"Sorry. Sometimes our residents take off for the winter. They don't always let us know they're gone or ask us to keep an eye on their place. As to the owner, you can find that information at City Hall."

That wasn't good enough. "Sir." I raised my voice and my chin. "We need to see if someone is inside. How do we go about that?"

He held up a hand. "Miss, I'll get to you in a moment." He turned back to O'Reilly. "As I was saying, if the house is vacant, City Hall will have the past owner's name, and maybe another address for them. You will keep us apprised of your movements in our area?"

"Yes. Of course. You'll be the first to hear."

The sergeant put on a great, big smile, and looked down at me from his pedestal on high. "As for you, little lady, the house is off limits. Without the owner there, the house can be entered only with court approval, and that is police business."

I said nothing more, but a plan was forming in my mind.

CHAPTER TWENTY-SEVEN

The ride back was quiet. I was deep in thought, digesting my plan. Was it feasible, or was I being dangerously foolish? All I knew was I had to do something.

Detective O'Reilly dropped Mary at her home in Elmhurst, a narrow two-family red-brick building with matching two-step stoops. It looked like all the other houses along the street, a replica of so many others built in Queens. A dull sun had begun its evening journey as it slipped out of sight between the tall chimneys and roofs.

Getting out of the car, Mary directed a smile at O'Reilly that would melt metal. "Thanks for the lift, Detective." Turning to me, she waved. "See you in the morning, Zelda." Her voice was soft. "Please don't feel bad. I just know we'll find Janice."

She was up the steps and inside her front door before I could answer. I slumped back in my seat, disappointed with the day. I'd hoped for a more productive outcome.

Detective O'Reilly brooded as he continued to my home.

"What did you see inside that house?" I asked.

"Only a bare room. It was too dark to see much else."

I frowned. I knew he couldn't get a search warrant immediately, but that wasn't good enough. What if Janice's life depended on being found? Every hour mattered. He must know that. I had to look in that old house, see for myself whether or not it was empty. Tonight, I would check it out.

We turned left onto Sixty-Third Street. An empty feeling hit me when I saw my house. What had we accomplished? Not a thing, yet I felt weary, like I'd climbed mountains, swam seas. My every bone ached.

As the car slowed to a halt, O'Reilly said, "Miss Bea, I'm putting Miss Bates back on the missing persons list. When I learn who the owner of the house is, I promise to let you know. If your friend is alive, we will find her and bring her home."

I assumed that was his apology for very little accomplished. My emotions snapped. "We just have to wait, is that it,

Detective? But what if Janice can't wait? What if every minute matters? And what if we are already too late?"

He said nothing, that invisible shield dropping over his face again.

I wanted to cry on his shoulder—on anybody's shoulder. I needed to be held, reassured. A feeling of helplessness swept over me. What could I really do? This latest lead was just a wild guess. What if Big Joe wasn't even involved?

Tomorrow, Jimmy would pick me up as usual, and I would go back to work at Federal. I swallowed hard at the thought of coming face to face with Big Joe again. What if he knew it was me driving the car that was following him? I had to be calm. After all, what could he do to me, out in the open with everybody around? I would play dumb and hope I could get away with it. He thought all women were dumb, anyway.

I looked back as O'Reilly turned his car around, then unlocked my door and went inside. I had to find something to eat.

I stared into my cupboard. A can of tuna fish. It would do. I mixed it with some mayo and slapped some of it on a slice of Levy's rye bread. I poured a glass of milk, forcing myself to stay awake as I chewed and sipped.

Perhaps a short nap before driving to Great Neck. I would be no use to anyone if I fell asleep driving.

I left the dishes in the sink. Still dressed, I lay down on top of my bed and drifted to sleep. The house in Great Neck took over my dreams. I was outside on the snow-covered driveway staring up at the empty dwelling. I climbed the three steps and walked to the front door. I turned the knob. It was unlocked. I walked in, stopped, and looked around, closing the door silently behind me. I strolled through rooms empty of furniture. I crept up squeaking attic steps, moving quietly. The door at the top was locked. I found the key over the doorframe, placed it in the keyhole, and turned it. Pushing the door open, I stared into a dark, forbidding space. In a far corner, I saw a cot with a body on it. Janice opened her eyes and looked up at me. "Who are you?"

A shrill sound woke me. Meow jumped on my head. I screamed. Then the sound rang again, piercing my ears. I groaned. The phone. I crawled out of bed and stumbled to the living room, reaching for the instrument.

"Hello," barely escaped my lips. I felt myself drifting back to sleep.

"Hello. Hello. Zelda?"

"Yes?"

"It's Sadie. I'm sorry to disturb you. I know you're up at this time for work. I wanted to catch you before you left."

My eyes searched for the clock on the table. It was nearly six o'clock in the morning? "Ohmygosh, I'm running late."

"I won't keep you long. It's just that Billy is crying. He wants to talk to you."

I heard a squeaky little voice. "Aunt Zelda? Where *are* you?"

Billy. I had meant to call him last night. How could I have slept through? "Hello, sweetie. Are you all right?"

"Yes, thank you." There was a pause, then, "Are you going away? Like my mommy?" His little voice had a quiver in it.

"No, Billy. I'm staying right here. And when I come home from work tonight, I'll tell you all about my day."

"Tonight? You will call me tonight? You promise?"

"I will call, Billy. I promise. But your gram needs your help right now. She's just home from the hospital."

"I know."

"And you are not to worry about me or your mom. We will all be together again soon."

"Really soon?"

What if I were wrong? But I can't be wrong. "Cross my heart. Everything will sort itself out, Billy. You'll see."

"Okay."

"I love you, Billy."

"Love you, too." And he was gone.

"Zelda?"

"Sadie. I'm glad you're home again. Is Billy too much for you?

"My boy?" She snorted. "He's no trouble. You gave him a smile again. And Ida is coming to visit this afternoon. She's such a nice lady. Have you heard anything about Janice?"

"Not yet, Sadie. I'm going to work now. I'll phone when I get home tonight."

"Bye, then." The phone clicked. Although she was a woman of few words, Sadie's tone spoke for her. She put on a brave show, but I heard her concern.

CHAPTER TWENTY-EIGHT

I threw my clothes in the hamper and showered. In fifteen minutes, I was in the kitchen dressed in fresh Levis and a clean flannel shirt, and drinking warmed-over coffee. As I sipped, I gazed out the frosty window. I had a decision to make—should I go to work or to the house in Great Neck?

By the time Jimmy's red Buick rolled to a stop, I knew Great Neck had won. I couldn't stand around waiting for Detective O'Reilly to decide what to do. After I checked out the house, I would drive to New Jersey. I would only be an hour late to work, and maybe I could refill my tank again. It was perfect.

I told Jimmy I had an errand to run. I would be taking my car today. Mary gave a little hiccup of alarm, but then seemed to swallow her words. I was glad she didn't try to tag along. I needed to do this myself.

I waved to them as they drove off then went back inside. I filled my small thermos with what coffee was left in the pot, tossed the grinds into the garbage, and washed the pot. I added a warm sweater under my fleece-lined leather jacket. I'd need it when I got to work. Besides, I might be searching the outside of the house, and it was cold on Long Island.

Picking up my car keys, I paused. Should I call Detective O'Reilly, let him know where I was going? No, it would be just like him to try to stop me.

I locked the front door. My plan was to look the house over, satisfy myself Janice was not there, and cross that one off our list of possibilities. At the very least, I would have eased the nagging thought that she was locked up in a deserted house.

And if you are there, dear friend, I will find you.

I drove carefully. My errand was too important to risk a speeding ticket or an accident. At this early hour, the roads going toward New York were busy. Cars moved at a steady, continuous pace. Not all Long Islanders were farmers. Many had jobs in the city. If it were the weekend, the traffic would be reversed. The roads going east would be busy even this early and out of season. Long Island, with the Sound and the ocean and the beaches, was a drawing-card even in wintertime. In summer, traffic going east moved inch-by-inch.

I made good time, turning left off the Queens-L.I. Expressway in less than twenty-five minutes. There I was, in Great Neck and turning onto Rabbit Run. It was a little after six-thirty in the morning.

The house presented itself like a Christmas card in the early morning light. Fresh snow carpeted the ground, all clean and white. Bare tree branches were dressed for a winter ball, stretching their limbs like they were showing off their coats of fur. It looked like it shouldn't be disturbed, so sweet and peaceful.

Yet my heart beat wildly. Taking a deep breath, I began to pull into the driveway, then stopped. No, I couldn't leave tracks. I was about to break into someone's home. I could go to jail if I were caught.

Instead, I parked in the copse of oak trees where I hid before. My wheels sank in the fresh snow. It was deeper than I had expected. Please, I prayed as I shut off the motor, don't let me get stuck. Don't let the wheels freeze in the snow before I leave.

My car was now tucked into a nest hidden by low branches. It should be safe enough. I opened my door. Then on impulse I brought along the thermos of coffee. If I found Janice, she might need the energy boost.

I stepped out. Through the trees, I saw the driveway. No footprints disturbed the pristine landscape. No one had entered or left the house since last night's snowfall.

I stopped at the edge of the trees, my gaze traveling to the front stoop. If I climbed the steps, my boots would make perfect prints in the fresh snow. If anyone came by, they would know someone had been snooping. There had to be another door.

I stayed in the trees flanking the edge of the property and made it to the remnants of a garden gone to winter sleep. The back door had four small glass panes. One had a board missing. I stepped to it. Shielding my eyes, I peered inside. The room was abandoned, empty. O'Reilly had not been lying. I reached for the knob and turned it. Just like in my dream, it opened.

I backed away as if I had touched hot coals. Was I still asleep?

Stop it. The door is unlocked, that's all. It's not so unusual. People leave back doors unlocked all the time. And thank you, God.

I entered the kitchen. Stepping lightly, I checked the rest of the house. The place was spotless, like it had been cleaned recently. In the living room, newspapers were piled neatly by a brick hearth. A small green scatter rug lay on the floor in front of it. But no furniture. No curtains. And no stairs that went up to an attic.

So much for my dream.

It took no time to walk through the small bedrooms. I checked the few closets. They were empty, not a solitary hanger. I backtracked to the kitchen and the rear door. Crushing disappointment engulfed me. I had wasted the morning.

As I turned to leave, I saw another door tucked next to the cabinets. Mentally crossing my fingers, I turned the knob. It was locked.

I searched for something, anything, to pry it open. The drawers were as empty as the rest of the house. But when I looked up, I saw a metal ring with a single key hanging from the doorjamb.

It was too high for me to reach. I needed something to stand on. I pulled out a drawer, set it upside down on the floor, and climbed aboard. Stretching on tip-toe, I managed to just touch the key. I flicked it, and the ring slipped off the nail it hung from and fell to the floor.

I jumped off the drawer, excitement tying a knot in my throat. I inserted the key into the lock. It entered as smooth as silk. The click it made sent tingles up my arm. I allowed myself to breathe again.

The brass knob felt cold as I turned it and pulled the door slowly toward me. Chilled, dank air struck my face. A cellar. Of course. I should have expected to find a cellar. All these houses had one.

Through the deep black of the doorway, I made out the top of a flight of stairs.

Placing my thermos on a counter, I held the door with one hand. With the other I felt for a light switch, a cord, something to light the way. I stepped onto the top step, eyes straining to adjust to the blackness of the windowless space, and I inched down.

Zelda the Welder

Something jarred her out of her stupor. She lifted her head, listening. Boxes surrounded her—the accumulation Big Joe brought in and added to every day. Sometimes she felt they were crowding in on her, taking her air, her space, what little she had. Her mind drifted. The young woman on the cot forced herself to concentrate, to keep awake.

There it was again, sounds coming from the stairway. Her heart pumped faster, responding to the new noise. Someone was coming down the steps. And it wasn't Big Joe Morgan—no, not him, with his heavy boots clomping loud and mean where they hit hardwood and then concrete floor.

She listened, remaining very still. There, again. She *had* heard it. A light tread, so different from Big Joe's. She wanted to call out, Who is it? Who's there?

But even if she found her voice, she would be afraid to speak. What if it were the others, those who wanted her dead? Big Joe said he was ordered to kill her, but he couldn't. Instead, he'd brought her here. Which was worse? This place was like a tomb, like she'd been buried alive.

Was she going to die? She winced with the thought, her heart about to burst with longing for her little boy. *Oh Billy, are you missing me? I know Gram will take good care of you. Please don't forget me.*

It was so dark, so hard to make out the shadowy silhouette that was emerging from the stairwell. Dare she call to them? Her tongue felt like it was stuck to the roof of her mouth. Her throat was so very dry it hurt to swallow. Each breath grew tighter.

If only she could make some noise. She would beg them to untie her, to let her go. She'd promise not to tell what she had seen. She'd tell them about her three-year-old son. Waiting. Was he waiting?

Hot tears trailed down the sides of her face, soaking the grimy pillow. She tried to move, but her muscles refused. They seemed atrophied. Even her feet felt like they didn't belong to her.

Was she dead? She couldn't be. She would feel nothing if she were dead.

The sound again. Someone was in the cellar. She tried to call out.

Just some water, please.

Only a low groan escaped her parched lips.

Zelda the Welder

I reached the bottom step, running my hand along the wall, hoping to find a switch, a cord, something that would light my way. I remembered the flashlight I kept in my car and turned to get it when I heard a low, guttural sound, more like a grunt.

My skin prickled. "Hello?"

No answer, just that sound again, so low I wondered if I'd really heard it.

My heart beat faster, and a powerful rush of blood rose to my face, flushed it hot. "Janice? Is that you?"

Again that muffled sound, a shade stronger this time.

I shuffled from the stairway, hands outstretched, one careful step at a time. My foot bumped something. I reached down, felt a soft, wooly object. A blanket?

Just then, I heard a door bang. I gasped, staring upward. Footsteps crossed the ceiling.

I had company.

CHAPTER TWENTY-NINE

My jaw clamped tight. Someone was in the kitchen directly above me. Their stride was long and loud, like a tall man wearing heavy boots. The footsteps stopped before reaching the cellar door, paused several moments, then retraced their steps to the back door. I hoped they were leaving. No such luck. The pacing was repeated several times before the sound ceased. It was quiet above.

And that's when I remembered that I had left my thermos of coffee on the kitchen counter. My eyes widened in the darkness, and a gasp huffed from my lips. I put my hand to my mouth, hoping to quiet the sound.

Something tugged my pant leg. I jumped back. "Who's there?" No answer.

Were there rats down here?

Footsteps creaked in the kitchen. I had to hide. I stretched out my arms as I moved away. My fingers touched a stack of shadowy squares. They felt like heavy, corrugated cardboard.

Boxes. Most of the basement was stacked with boxes. They were everywhere, piled one atop the other, reaching nearly to the ceiling.

I heard footsteps again, then a creak as the cellar door opened.

Oh, no. I'd left it unlocked, left the key in the keyhole. Frantic, I glanced around. *Hide. Hide.*

A flashlight beam traveled from the top step to the cellar floor. In the scant light, I saw I had just enough room to squeeze my body between the wall and the boxes. I sucked in my breath, sidestepping until I was under cover.

Careful. Careful. Don't knock anything over.

The wooden staircase groaned with a heavy stomp of boots. Someone big was making their way down. The high beam of a flashlight danced over the room. It hit the slim crack between the boxes I hid behind, blinding me as much as the darkness had earlier.

I gulped and pressed against the wall. Memories of the last time I hid behind boxes flashed before me. I had been in the shed on the top deck of the DE. Was it just a few days ago? It seemed longer. I had been frightened then, but that didn't come near to how terrified I was at this moment.

The flare of light moved away. I peered through a thin opening between my stack of boxes and the next one. There was a cot. I saw it clearer now. I made out what looked like a body lying there. My blood raced.

Janice?

Then, close to where I stood, a light bulb on a long cord was switched on. Its dim glow drew a wide circle as it twisted in the air, highlighting the cot and the person lying prone upon it.

It *was* Janice. She *was* here. I bit down hard to keep from calling out, from moving to her.

The surrounding area came to light. Unfinished beams on the walls and ceiling stood out in their nakedness. Spider webs filled the niches, adding to the horror. Dust layered the webs, the wood, the floor. And everywhere were boxes. Stacks and stacks.

I shivered, but not from the chill. I shivered for Janice. Her hands and feet were bound, and she was trapped and alone in this horrible place.

My gaze followed the swinging light, and I stood stock-still, terrified I'd make a noise. Big Joe stood so close I could reach out and touch him.

Seeing him didn't surprise me. It did frighten me. Bringing my hands down from my face, I clenched them tightly, my nails cutting into my palms. I concentrated on the pain to keep from sobbing.

My eyes went back to Janice lying on the narrow canvas bed. She looked so fragile. Her beautiful red hair, once smooth and gleaming, now lay in a snarled mass like on Billy's beloved Raggedy Ann doll. Her face was pinched, blotchy. My always-immaculate friend's heavy Levis were now twisted and crumpled under her. She had on her lined winter jacket, without which she would have frozen in this unheated, morbid place. She lay on her back, her arms tied in front of her, legs spread, ankles attached to each side of the cot.

I heard her speak, her crackly voice almost inaudible. "Water?"

My heart ached. I wanted to get her out of this disgusting hellhole.

"Sure, kid. Gimme a minute," Joe said with a grin in his voice.

That was Big Joe being nice. His arms were filled with boxes which he now piled on top of others. I peeked through the narrow space and watched him arrange them in lines in front of the pile I crouched behind. He went back upstairs several times, always returning with more boxes. Except for the small area Janice was in and a path to the staircase, the basement was filled. On his last trip he carried a brown paper bag, which he placed on the cot.

He sat next to Janice. From the pocket of his jacket, he brought out a red thermos bottle. The sight of it reminded me again that I had left mine upstairs on a counter in the kitchen. All I could do now was pray he hadn't seen it.

"I brought you a treat, kid," Big Joe said. "Some of my special coffee. Careful, it's hot."

I remembered his special coffee—spiked with whiskey. He poured some into the thermos cup. It steamed in the cold air. Then he lifted Janice's head, helping her drink. With her hands still tied, Janice clutched the cup, drinking thirstily.

Every so often Joe darted a glance around, questions wrinkling his expression. What was he looking for? Had he seen my thermos? Could he sense someone was there, hiding?

Big Joe took away the cup. He reached into the bag and brought out a sandwich wrapped in crinkly waxed paper. Setting it on the bed, he then untied her hands.

Janice was made to sit up. Her face stood out, so tired looking. A tear rolled down her cheek. A lock of hair dangled over one eye. She seemed too weak to brush it away. Joe tore open the sandwich wrapper, broke off a bit of bread, and held it out to her. She fumbled for it. Taking a small bite, she chewed slowly.

"You must think I'm a monster," Big Joe said. "Isn't that what you called me before? A monster? But I'm taking care of you, ain't I? I brought you here to keep you safe, didn't I? If the boss knew you were still alive, we'd both be dead. Trust me, doll. As soon as we can sell this last bit of inventory, we'll be gone. They'll never catch us then. And you can go free. It won't be long now."

The grin spreading over his handsome face sickened me. It was all I could do not to yell ugly words at him as his long arms reached for her. She looked so tiny beside him. I wanted to jump out and smash the grin off his face.

She winced as he turned her toward him.

"My red-haired beauty." His voice changed, grew softer, tender. "Hold on a second." He untied her ankles. Her legs were free. He bent her knees and rubbed her feet a short while, then up to her thighs. "That better?"

I saw her jaw clench, her lips press tight.

He took her in his arms, bending her head to his. The kiss went on and on, his large hands reaching beneath her jacket, roving her body.

I couldn't watch such a disgusting display. My stomach curdled. I was afraid I was going to be sick. I turned abruptly, bringing my hand to my mouth. My elbow knocked a box askew. It brushed against another, and another. The towering stacks teetered. As if in slow motion, they fell, dumping their contents to the floor.

Zelda the Welder

I scrunched low, creeping along the wall, keeping from sight as a chain reaction knocked over more and more boxes. As the mass toppled, the crashing became louder. I held my ears, forcing myself not to scream, not to dash from my cover.

"What the hell?" Big Joe bellowed. There came a strangled cry from Janice as he pushed her out of his way and got to his feet.

I hid behind the last two piles, my back to the wall, my vision locked on what was going on beyond the small opening. I saw Joe approach, looking thunderstruck. Behind him, I saw Janice pull herself from the cot and inch her way toward the stairs. It had been a while since she walked, and she could barely hobble towards the stairway. Wearing only socks, her feet made no sound.

Mentally, I called out to her. *Run, Janice, run. Don't stop.* I crouched lower, getting set to make my dash for the exit.

But Big Joe stopped right before me, staring at the mess littering the floor. He stood much too close to where I knelt concealed behind the remaining boxes. Janice gasped, and he looked back at her. I could almost see his mind whirling—which way to go? Toward his precious boxes? To Janice to stop her?

Several boxes had split open when they fell, the contents spilling out. I saw now why they were so heavy. Pieces of metal scattered over the floor. Scrap metal! From the shipyard!

He was less than a foot from me. Surely he could hear my heart pounding like a drummer on parade as I reached for one of the sections of steel from the broken box. I chose a long piece. It was heavier than I expected. I nearly dropped it. I had no time to think. Big Joe looked toward Janice as she limped up the stairway. It was now or not at all. Holding the metal rod in both hands, I stepped out from my hiding place. With all the strength I could muster, I hit him low on the back of the head. My aim was true. He slid quietly to the floor.

I looked down at him, then I ran—dropping the weapon. I heard it clang, heard it bounce a few times on the cement floor. Big Joe didn't move. I hoped I had just knocked him out.

He couldn't be dead. Please, don't let him be dead.

Zelda the Welder

I reached Janice on the stairs. Half carrying, half pulling, I drew her up the flight of steps. As I passed the kitchen counter, I grabbed my thermos. Then I pushed through the back door, running into the snow-covered yard.

Janice wheezed and stumbled.

She frightened me. I had never seen anyone so abused before. "Please, Jan. Don't stop now. He's not dead. He's just out. We have to keep moving."

I panted like I had just run a mile as we pushed through the line of trees that bordered the yard. Clumps of new snow plopped down from above, leaving us cold and wet. I didn't care. I had found Janice. She was alive.

Billy's concerned little face flashed before me. *It's okay, Billy. See, I kept my promise. Your mom will be home soon.*

My car stood tucked in its little niche just as I'd left it. No one had found it. I wrenched open the passenger door, then settled Janice on the seat.

Handing her the thermos, I said, "Drink."

I pulled off her wet socks. Wresting the blanket from the back, I wrapped its dry warmth around her and tucked her wet feet in tight.

I closed the passenger door then sprinted for the driver's side, sliding behind the wheel. I turned the key in the ignition, and the motor rumbled. *Thank you, God.* I looked over at Janice and patted her knee.

She curled up against the door, eyes wide, staring out the window into the small, white forest we had just run through. In a low, barely audible voice, she said, "I hope he's dead."

CHAPTER THIRTY

This was the moment to cheer. Only I couldn't. I had no cheer in me, just a small, gray cloud. I was almost sure Big Joe wasn't dead. "He's lying unconscious on the cellar floor. When he wakes up, he'll be mad as hell." I gulped. "He isn't dead."

I backed the car from the niche of trees, easing it onto the narrow road. The feeling that I had lived this moment before swept over me, only this time Big Joe didn't come tearing through the stand of oak.

Don't let him be dead.

I sailed down Rabbit Run at fifty miles an hour, my insides still shaking.

Janice drank hot coffee from the thermos. "Zelda," she croaked. "Thank you."

With my hands steady on the wheel, I sat back and breathed, calming the wild turmoil inside. Amazed at myself, I said, "We made it out. We did it!"

There was time now to absorb the realization of what I had done. I'd found her. Despite all the people who told me I was wrong. Janice was safe beside me in the car. She wasn't dead. She was very much alive. I should be over the moon.

But Janice coughed and sputtered weakly.

I glanced warily at her. "Janice, I think you should see a doctor before we do anything else."

"No. No doctor." She closed her eyes. "Billy."

I drove faster. I didn't know what else to do. Janice had been starved, locked in a dank and dirty basement, afraid for her very life. She needed to see a doctor. I should take her to a hospital, despite what she said. But she looked so frail. I didn't want to upset her further. I had no choice but to drive straight home.

Fifteen minutes later, I pulled onto 63rd Street, drove the short half-block to my house, parked, and turned off the ignition. As I removed the key, Janice moaned. One hand over her mouth, she jerked open the door, leaned out, and threw up on the snow bank.

I jumped out of my side of the car and ran around to her. "Oh, my poor Janice."

I heard a faint, "Yuck."

"You poor thing. I'm so sorry. I thought the coffee would help."

"You did help." She sat sideways in the seat, half in, half out, holding her drooping head in her hands like she never wanted to move again.

I gently pushed her hair off her damp forehead. She smiled a thank you.

"It's cold out here," I told her. "Come inside. You'll be more comfortable. I'll make you some soup."

"All right."

Hooking my arm beneath hers, I helped her up, avoiding the sick in the snow. Holding her firmly against me, I guided her to my door. When we got inside, Meow made a figure-eight around our legs, nearly tripping us. I managed to get her to the couch. She collapsed more than sat. I ran back to close and lock the door. Then I pulled off her jacket.

She smelled horrible, like she'd been denied the use of a toilet. I hurried to the bathroom and dampened a facecloth in the sink. Returning to my friend, I patted her face and mouth.

She blinked and jerked her head as if I'd startled her awake. "I have to get home."

"Once Big Joe wakes up and finds you gone, the first place he'll think to look is your apartment."

Janice's face turned somber, eyes widening with fear. "Please. My son. My mother."

Oh God. I hadn't thought of that. Now they were in danger, too. "What if I bring them here?"

"What if he saw you?"

I stood, dropping the damp cloth to the floor. She was right. If Big Joe put two and two together, he might come darkening my door. What should I do?

Grabbing the phone, I dialed Ida's number.

She picked up on the first ring. "Hello."

"Ida."

"I knew it was you. I saw you pull up. Who is that with you?"

I cringed from the question. You never knew who might be listening in on the three-party line. "Can you come over for coffee?"

"Be right there."

I hung up the phone. Janice groaned. She placed a hand over her mouth. I got her up and guided her to my bathroom. I left her leaning over the commode and went into the kitchen. I started coffee for Ida and opened a can of Campbell's Chicken Noodle Soup for Janice.

The doorbell rang, and I peeked out the window. It was Ida.

"Your door was locked," she complained.

I pulled her inside and locked up behind her.

She looked alarmed. "Now can you tell me what is going on?"

"I have Janice," I blurted. "I found her, Ida. I rescued her. It was pure luck."

"Janice is with you?"

"Yes. But she can't stay here." I took a breath and said, "I have a gigantic favor to ask."

"Whatever I can do. You know that."

"I need you to take Billy, Sadie, and Janice for a couple of days."

Her face lit. "I would enjoy that. I'm anxious to meet Janice. And I'll have my little darling visiting again." Ida looked around. "But where are they? Where is your friend? And why do I think there is something you're not telling me?"

I turned toward a small sound. Janice stood in the doorway.

Ida gasped. "Oh, my Lord."

I took Janice's arm. "Come lie down on the couch."

"I've had enough lying down." She gave me a brave, trembling smile. "I'll just sit in this chair."

I helped her into the chair next to the radio. Then I stepped beside Ida. "It's time you two were introduced. Ida, this is Janice Bates, Billy's mom. Janice, this is our guardian angel, Ida. She cared for Billy while I was at work."

Janice frowned. "Billy was here? Where was my mother?"

"Sadie had a heart attack. She was so worried when we couldn't find you. The strain was too much." I perked up. "But she's home now. She's fine."

Janice listened, twisting her hands in her lap like the raw spots on her wrists pained her. "She's always been so strong. I never thought my mother would fall ill."

I said, "Anyway, Ida watched Billy when Sadie was in the hospital. He listened to *The Lone Ranger* with her."

Janice nodded. I saw how she tried to smile, but her weariness showed in the dark circles around her eyes, her gaunt face, and her emaciated body. In a croaking voice, she said, "Thank you, Ida, for taking care of my son."

Ida beamed. "It is my pleasure to know Billy. He's very special. Just what this old lady needed."

I snapped my fingers. "Soup."

I hurried to the kitchen. The coffee had just started to bubble, and I watched it through the small, round, glass top on the percolator. The kitchen filled with that wonderful morning-aroma of fresh coffee. The soup was also bubbling. I gave it a stir and ladled some into a mug, trying to get more broth than noodles.

Ida followed me. "Your friend needs a hospital."

"She won't go."

"The police, then. Someone needs to answer for what's been done to her."

I thought of Detective O'Reilly. For all the good he's done. "I'll call them next. Want some coffee?"

Ida took down three cups and poured the fresh brew.

I glanced at my watch. The morning was moving on. I had better get Janice settled so I could leave for work. I had planned to get to Federal before noon. I picked up a coffee cup and the mug of soup and carried them into the living room.

Janice accepted the mug with both hands and sipped noisily. Her lined face eased into a smile. "So good."

"I think we should call the police now," I told her. "They've been looking for you. They need to know you've been found. And we have to tell them that Big Joe might be after you."

"No police." Janice shook her head. "I have to get my son."

"It wouldn't be smart to take you to your apartment, not for Billy or Sadie or you. I'll get them. You'll all be safer at Ida's house. She'll get some good food into you, I promise."

Her eyes sparkled with tears. "You'll bring them to me?"

Zelda the Welder

"I'll call them now." I rang their house. I waited for what seemed like several minutes. I was about to hang up when I heard a tiny voice squeak, "Hello?"

"Billy? Is that you?"

"Aunt Zelda," his small voice screeched. "Aunt Zelda, you coming here?"

"Yes, I am."

Janice held out her hand, her arm shaky, tears rolling down her cheeks.

I said, "Billy, I have someone who wants to talk to you. Hold on." I passed the phone to Janice.

Eagerly, she grabbed the telephone from my hand. "Hello? Can this be Billy Bates, the young man I love?"

"Mommy!"

I heard his cry from where I stood, his joy booming.

Janice's lip trembled. "Oh, Billy. How are you, darling?"

Smiling, I bent close, and Janice tilted the receiver so that I might hear him.

"Mommy. You coming home? You coming home now?"

"Aunt Zelda is going to bring you and Gram to me. Can I speak to Gram now, please?"

"Gram! Mommy! Here!" His voice rose with each word.

There was a short pause. Then I heard, "Janice? Is that you? Where are you? Where have you been? What happened to you?"

"Ma. Listen. Pack a few things for you and Billy and me. Just enough for a couple days. I'll explain when I see you."

Through the phone, I heard Sadie's sharp tone. "That's all you can tell me? What's happening?"

Janice looked like she could fall over at any minute.

I took the phone from her. "Sadie, do as Janice says. Please. It's for her safety and yours. I'll be by to pick you up."

I waited for an answer. Then she said, "I'll do it, but you better have a good reason. All this is scary for an old lady."

"See you within the hour." I placed the earpiece in its holder, wondering when all the intrigue was going to end and my life would return to normal.

CHAPTER THIRTY-ONE

I sat with Ida on the couch while Janice gulped the rest of her soup.

She sighed and leaned back. Then she touched her hair, trying to pull her fingers through the tangles. "I can't let them see me like this. I need a shower."

"Are you sure you're strong enough?"

"Are you kidding?" Her face looked transformed. "I could fly."

"Then let me fly you into the bathroom and get you started." I took a firm hold on her arm and helped her walk. Once there, I turned on the water and adjusted the temperature. "There you go. I'll find some clothes for you to change into."

She'd had on the same work clothes for days, rumpled and smelly. They should be tossed out or scrubbed clean in boiling water. And that jacket was past redemption.

I rifled through my closet, searching for something warm and comfortable. I took out a long, black wool skirt and a warm red sweater that would do nicely. Long stockings and undies were next. I found a pair of boots I knew she'd like. We were lucky to wear the same sizes.

I winced when I thought of her poor neglected hair. It needed a good wash. I gathered shampoo and a fresh bar of Ivory soap. If I'd had brown soap, I would have scrubbed her with it.

She was already in the shower when I brought the things into the bathroom. I moved the shower curtain enough to hand her the soap and shampoo.

"Your clothes are right here," I called as I hung her clean clothes on the towel rack.

I closed the bathroom door and went looking for Ida. She was washing the coffee cups.

"That poor woman," Ida said.

"I know. I feel awful for her. The worst part is if I could have gotten anyone to believe me she might have been found that much sooner."

"You can't blame yourself. You did all you could. I'd say you saved her life."

"Still… I just wish…"

Ida came over and hugged me tight. Tears sprang to my eyes. I wanted to just stay there wrapped in her warmth.

She patted my shoulder and stepped away. "You're a good friend. We're all lucky to have you."

I sniffled, pulling myself together. "I'd better go pick up Sadie and Billy. When Janice gets out of the shower, you two should go across to your place and wait there. I'll feel better if I know you're both safe. After I drop the others off, I have to go to work. I'll tell them I had to pick Sadie up at—"

The doorbell rang. My heart jumped like it would burst through my skin. Ida let out a squeak as her hand flew to her mouth.

I stared blankly. "Who would be ringing my doorbell? No one would expect me home at this hour."

I felt the panic build as I rushed into the living room. Janice came out of the bathroom wearing my clothes and a towel around her hair.

Grabbing her hand, I searched for a place to hide her. *Behind the couch. Yes, that would have to do.* I pointed. "Please. Go there."

She nodded and got down on her hands and knees. I waited until she had squeezed out of sight.

My heart thumped as the impatient caller rang several more times. With my legs unsteady and my hands shaking, I went to answer the door. Parting the curtain a hair, I peeked through.

Sadie stood on my stoop holding Billy in her arms as he rang my bell. His grin seemed to cover his entire cherub face.

Sighing with relief, I called, "It's okay."

I opened the door wide, hugged them both, and ushered them in. Stepping around them, I looked outside. A taxi sat parked behind my car. I glanced up and down the street. It was empty. Everyone was at work this time of day. I closed the door and locked it.

"What?" Sadie asked. "What's all the looking for? Don't lock the door. Our suitcases are in the cab. You need to get them and pay the driver."

"Oh, Sadie. You scared the non-sense out of me. What happened? I was supposed to go for you. Our paths might have crossed *en route*."

"I thought it would be better if I called a taxi. I didn't want to wait."

I wanted to laugh, to cry. Instead, I hugged her. I unlocked the door and called out, "Just a moment," and went for my purse.

Billy stood in the middle of the front hall. "Aunt Zelda, where's Mommy?"

There was a rustling sound, and Janice popped out from behind the couch, laughing. "Oh Billy, here I am, darling."

With a cry of glee, he rushed into her arms.

My eyes clouded up. I never wanted to forget the moment.

I stepped out the door as the taxi driver walked up carrying two suitcases. I smiled and tipped him generously. "Thank you."

Sadie was right, this did save me some time, but it was a silly thing to do. I glanced at my watch. If nothing further happened, I would get to work before noon. Good.

I locked the door and returned to the living room. Ida sat on the couch.

Sadie embraced her daughter. "You better have a good explanation for all this."

Janice sat in the chair. Billy crawled into her lap and snuggled against her. She looked at me. "May I have some water, please?"

"Of course." I hurried into the kitchen, filled a glass from the tap, then carried it to her.

She took a sip. In a slow, tired voice, she said, "I was abducted and held prisoner in a cellar with very little access to food or water." She held out a hand, showing her red, raw wrist. Her voice cracked and trembled. "I was tied."

Sadie gasped, covering her mouth with her hands. She sank onto the couch. "But why? How could this happen?"

I sat next to Sadie with my arm about her shoulders. "Yes, Janice. What started all this?"

She sipped again. "I was at work. I went into a shed on the top of a destroyer escort. I was looking for you, Zelda. I thought you might have gone inside to get out of the cold. Instead, I found Big Joe. He was packing something into a duffle bag. He got angry at me. Angrier than I'd ever seen him. We struggled, and I fell. I must have hit my head." She touched her temple.

I thought of the trail of blood I'd found. If only I'd gotten someone to listen to me.

"When I woke, I was all doubled up inside the bag. I couldn't get free. It was so cold. I didn't know it then, but I was in the trunk of a car. After a while, I heard voices. I'd recognize them anywhere. Joe Morgan and Fen Hansen. They were talking about me, saying I knew too much."

"Hold it," I said. "Mr. Hansen, our boss, is in on this, too?"

Sadie said, "But what did you know, sweetheart?"

Janice's voice cracked as she blurted, "They're stealing. From the Yard."

"Stealing?" I remembered metal spilling from the boxes as they fell. "Scrap metal?"

"There are big bucks in nonferrous scrap metal. All the countries use it. Remember before the war, when we were selling our scrap to China? Well, it is still needed, now more than ever. Every day, the Yard gets huge shipments of metal. They have to cut the plates to fit. Big Joe steals the small, cut-up bits. The lighter metals are sorted and sealed in boxes in the small shacks on the decks. When he gets enough, Joe takes them to the house. Fen Hansen has the larger pieces crated up. No one questions the boss when he says to crate up something. Then he takes the scrap to some warehouse. Between them, Joe with boxes of the lighter stuff and Fen with one or two crates each night, the haul is worth a lot of money. Big Joe and Hansen were talking millions."

I whistled. "I knew Big Joe was sleazy, but—"

"There is a third man, too, but I don't know who he is. They referred to him as O. Like, O said this, and O said that."

"You say they have crates of the stuff?"

She nodded. "It's true. I heard them. Their plan is to empty the cellar and the warehouse as soon as they're full, take the money, and run. They said they have a buyer waiting."

"They might get away with it, too. Who would think to look in Great Neck for stolen metal?"

Janice took another gulp of water. She kissed the top of Billy's head. Quietly, she said, "Big Joe told me Fen ordered him to shut me up. Permanently."

"Oh, Janice," Sadie said.

"What happened?" I asked.

"Lucky me. Joe said he was too sweet on me for killing. Said he cared."

"Hell of a way to care," I said. "You look terrible."

Her mouth twisted like she was going to cry, tears already damp on her cheeks. Voice low, she said, "I'm so glad you were there. I don't want to think what would have happened if you hadn't knocked over those boxes."

"I hadn't planned it, but amen to that. You won't be safe until we get those characters into custody. I'll call O'Reilly, the detective on the case."

She took a sharp breath. "Detective? You're bringing in a detective?"

"Of course. We've been looking for you since you disappeared."

"The fellow, O. Mr. Hansen said everything would be all right because O was a cop. Then he laughed."

I blinked and stammered, "Th-their O is a p-policeman? What more do you know of him? Like maybe where he works?"

"They didn't say much, except he handled the money part, the connections."

"And they said this O person was with the police?"

I was troubled. I had planned to call O'Reilly. Now I wasn't sure. I hoped it was only a coincidence, a policeman called O, but I couldn't chance it. Not now. Too much had happened. I had to know more.

I turned to the older woman. "Sadie, Ida has invited you, Billy, and Janice to her house for a few days. I accepted for you. You'll love her cooking." She stared at me, and I knew she was going to balk. "It's a safety precaution, until we can clear up this mess." I smiled at the little boy watching me from Janice's lap, his expression serious. "Billy?"

His eyes lit, and he grinned. "I'll be good."

"I'm sure you will."

"Now what?" Ida asked, speaking for the first time since she sat down.

I sighed. I needed to think about how to protect Janice and her family. But I wasn't sure who to trust. Telling the police had been my first choice, but there was a policeman out there they called O, and I couldn't take the chance. Especially now, while we were not sure where Big Joe was. Or if he was alive or dead, for that matter.

"Now, we get you all to Ida's house. Then I have to show up at work. I said I'd be in, and I wouldn't want them to connect me with this morning's fun and games."

I had the grace to grin at that quip.

CHAPTER THIRTY-TWO

Smiling, I helped bundle Billy back into his coat. It was a short walk across the street to Ida's, but it wouldn't do to gamble with his health. I lent a long coat to Janice. One with a hood. It would help hide her face from prying eyes. Besides, her hair was still damp.

We crossed the street like we were on parade. Ida held Billy's hand. Janice leaned on Sadie. I locked my house and followed the progression. My breath billowed before me. Even that short distance chilled my bones.

We tumbled through the door. Ida's small house was warm and inviting.

"I hope we won't be an imposition," Sadie said as she took off her coat.

"Nonsense." Ida smiled, her eyes twinkling. "It will be cozy. We'll have a lovely time, you'll see."

I truly believed she was enjoying the company in spite of the circumstances. I knew she would do her best to keep my friends safe.

"I'd better get going," I said.

"Have you eaten?" Ida said. "At least let me make you a lunch."

"I'll grab something there. They usually have vendors at the gates. If I'm lucky they haven't left yet." I showed my crossed fingers. "So long, everybody. Wish me luck." And I was out the door.

As soon as I was out of sight, my smile disappeared. I worried about my friend's health and safety, worried that I had no one to turn to for help. I was overwhelmed with the knowledge that I may have killed a man, sleazy as Big Joe was.

The roads were clear at that hour, and I drove faster than usual. As I rolled along, I switched on my portable radio. The music would soothe me. Frank Sinatra sang a medley of tunes. One of my favorites, *I'll Never Smile Again,* conjured up memories of a very special guy overseas. When that song ended, Sinatra went into *Night and Day,* its lyrics resonating in me, another memory-catcher.

I swallowed a lump in my throat large enough to choke me. A tear flowed down my cheek. I rubbed at it with my cuff. Tender moments. I tried not to think of all those young GIs putting their lives out there for us. I couldn't break down now. There was too much at stake right here in Maspeth.

Sinatra finished, and the Mills Brothers' melodic voices filled the small car, singing *I'm gonna buy a paper doll that I can call my own*— when the song was interrupted by a news flash on the war in Europe. There had been a major strike on the shores of Sicily, and we had taken the island. The announcer's monotone voice went on to say casualties were many as the army advanced, crossing onto the boot of Italy.

I thought of one special GI somewhere overseas in this damned, destructive, dismal war, and I switched off the radio. I'd heard enough. Even the radio wouldn't give me a break.

One hour and forty minutes later, I reached the parking lot of Kearny Federal Shipyard. My luck held—there were still several vendors set up outside the gate. I bought a box lunch and pulled into the lot, parking in the back. I was almost out of gas. I'd have to get another voucher. I grabbed my lunch and hurried into the yard. It wasn't noon yet, and most everybody was still at work.

I got my gear and walked over to a fire barrel. Annie was there, warming her frosty hands.

"Cold today, eh?" I said.

She stared at me. "When did you get here? Where did you go? Mary is acting awfully mysterious. What have you two been up to?"

"I'll explain later. Has Big Joe been around?"

"No. Steve is giving out assignments. Better check with him. He'll want to know what kept you."

"I told you this morning I had to run an errand." I cleared my throat. "I drove Janice's mother home." It was almost true.

The rest of the morning was routine. I got my assignment from Steve and started work. Big Joe was nowhere to be seen. I tried to concentrate, although the picture of him lying on the floor of the cellar was never far from my thoughts.

Please, don't let him be dead, I prayed as I worked.

Then, in mid-afternoon, I saw him. For a moment, I felt lightheaded with relief. He was talking to some of the girls, and he sported a small, white bandage on the back of his head. It stood out neatly just below his black wool hat. His usual leering grin was gone. He didn't look happy at all. His overall expression was anxious, worried, eyes darting everywhere. Thank God I hadn't killed him. I couldn't stand that on my conscience.

He looked my way twice, yet he didn't come near me. That had to mean something. Was he biding his time to accuse me in private? Did he even realize I was involved? Perhaps he had no idea who had hit him. Maybe he thought it was just another falling box.

I shrugged him from my thoughts. There were more important issues to figure out. I still felt Janice should see a doctor. But if I took her to a hospital, they would report her condition to the police. I'd get in trouble for not letting the police know I'd found her.

And what of the policeman known by the letter O? What of Detective O'Reilly?

Zelda the Welder

We had to get Janice's story told. No one should abuse another person like that. And we had to stop the pilfering of materials. This metal belonged to the nation and our military. It was not up for grabs.

I was putting a neat bead on a piece of flat deck when the idea came to me. There *was* one person I felt I could trust with such a story. Hopefully, she would remember me—and her promise.

I finished my weld then put my rod and bucket aside. I had to find a phone. I would take my break now.

The office was busy as I entered. I hoped the noise would cover my conversation. I walked to the public telephone. Taking a deep breath, I asked the operator to put me through to the White House in Washington D.C. The phone rang several times.

Then, "Hello. Whom may I connect you with?"

"I am calling from New Jersey. I would like to talk to Mrs. Roosevelt, please."

There was a click. Then a sweet voice said, "Mrs. Roosevelt's suite. Whom shall I say is calling?"

"Tell her it is Zelda Bea from Kearny Federal Shipyard. She will want to speak with me."

"Oh. Miss Bea. Of course. I want to thank you for helping Mrs. Roosevelt. I'll put you through right away. One moment, please."

A tiny gasp escaped me when, a short time later, I heard the high-pitched voice of Eleanor Roosevelt. I was talking to the First Lady of the Land.

"Yes? Zelda? Hello, my dear girl."

CHAPTER THIRTY-THREE

Suddenly I felt foolish and tongue-tied. "Hello, Mrs. Roosevelt. I was concerned. I hope you weren't hurt in the fall."

"It is lovely of you to call. Why, I am just fine, only a couple of scratches, nothing broken. Otherwise, I'm good as new." She chuckled.

"I'm so glad." I paused a moment. How to begin? Plunge right in. "I'm taking you up on your invitation. I need to ask a favor."

Had I really asked the President's wife for a favor? Serve me right if she laughed.

A moment later I heard, "My dear, I would be glad to be of help, if I can."

To shut out the noises in the office, I held my hand over my left ear, and held the earpiece tight against my right one. I breathed deeply and began. "It concerns a friend of mine, Janice Bates. She's a welder at the Yard. Last week, we were to work together on the top deck of a DE. She never showed up. No one knew where she was. Not her fellow workers, not her mother, not her small son. No one had heard from her."

"My dear, did you call the police?"

"Yes. I personally was in touch with a detective in the Kearny precinct. He's been investigating her disappearance, or so he says. So far he claims to have drawn a blank."

"I see. And now you think I might help you find her when the police cannot?"

"No, I found her. This morning. I followed a lead to where she might be. I was right to be concerned. She had been kidnapped. She was alone, tied up, and locked in a dark cellar with little food or water. But I can't tell the police. Not yet. I don't know if one of theirs is involved."

Mrs. Roosevelt was silent at the other end.

I began again. "I know. It sounds like a line out of a detective novel. But it is true. When you hear the whole story, perhaps you'll know what I should do."

Her voice was patient, measured. "Well, why don't you tell me all you know, my dear?"

"Yes." I paused. How to say it? I didn't want to miss a point. "Janice found out about theft going on at the Yard. We work with some of the people involved. She told me one of her captors wanted her killed to keep her quiet. Fortunately, the other one didn't. Perhaps he thought he was being kind when he hid her from his buddy, but the place was deplorable. She looked terrible when I found her."

"And you don't think you should notify the police?"

"I think a police officer may be the ringleader. You're the only one I feel safe to tell about the theft, the thieves. Janice is safe for the moment. I brought her mother and son to be with her, for their safety as well as hers. But the thieves want her dead, knowing what she does. We need help, and soon." I crossed my fingers. "I remembered your kind words, if I ever needed you—" The quiet at the other end was palpable. "Can you help us?"

I waited some more.

Finally, I heard the familiar, high-pitched voice. "I do need to hear the whole story. Perhaps you can come to the White House. I will be home the next two days."

The White House? My mind whirled. In a small voice, I said, "I'm sure I can."

"Good. I will have a car waiting for you at the station, and my chauffer will drive you from the train to the White House. You can tell me then what this is all about."

"Yes. I will be ready."

"Shall we say tomorrow morning? You will need to know what time and which train to take."

"I'll do whatever is necessary."

"Let me put Missy on. She will take your information and get back to you as soon as everything is arranged. And, Zelda, I am pleased you called. I hope I can help you and your friend. Goodbye, my dear. I will see you tomorrow."

She was gone, and in her place the same sweet-sounding voice I first spoke to asked me several questions. I gave her the number of the public telephone I was using and my address. She said she would call me within the hour with the train times.

I paced the office. I glanced around the busy room, at the big clock on the wall, a dozen times at my watch. Did I have a moment to get a cup of coffee? I ran across to the employee cafeteria. An eternity passed as I waited in line to pay at the checkout.

With my coffee in hand, I returned to the office. I needed to get back to work. Ring phone, ring, I pleaded silently.

I waited.

Forty minutes had passed when the phone rang. I jumped, spilling my cooling brew. I put the cup down and picked up the earpiece. "Hello," I said, so nervously soft I cleared my throat and said again, "Hello?"

"I've purchased your tickets," Missy told me. "Everything is arranged. A car will be at your door at six-thirty a.m. and will take you to Grand Central Station. You will be in the city by seven-thirty a.m. The train should leave at eight o'clock. Just give your name to the ticket agent, and he will give you your boarding pass and return ticket. Mrs. Roosevelt expects you for lunch."

"Thank you. Please thank Mrs. Roosevelt for me. Tell her I am looking forward to seeing her tomorrow." I stood there like I couldn't come down off the cloud I found myself on. I was to have lunch with that wonderful woman who traveled all over the world. She was so busy, and she was finding the time to help *me* on her day off. Slowly, I replaced the receiver. I would never forget this moment.

I returned to the ship I had been working on, picked up my rod and bucket, and continued welding where I had left off. I expected Big Joe to blast me for being away from the job so long, but I did not see him again. I heaved a sigh of thanks.

I made record time getting home, heading straight for Ida's house. It felt wonderful to finally be there. Everyone was as happy to see me as I was to see them. Janice looked stronger. Billy was never far from her side, always touching her as if to reassure himself that she was home. I think Janice felt the same way.

We sat down to a dinner of stuffed cabbages and mashed potatoes. The red sweet-and-sour gravy was perfect. I was ready for an early night and sleep after Ida's really super meal. But I couldn't say goodnight until I told my friends about my invitation from Madam Roosevelt and my plans for the next day. They rewarded me with gasps and smiles.

Janice's sunken eyes lit up as she put into words what I knew they were all thinking. "Zelda at the White House. What a great honor."

"One thing," I said, "No one else must know. Just say that I had an errand to run. That's all I told them at work. It's the only way to keep you all safe."

Billy sat in the chair next to me, his mom on his other side. He looked up at me, cheeks stuffed with food, and nodded, eyes wide. He managed a tiny smile. I knew he understood the importance of my little speech. Grinning back, I ruffled his hair.

I turned to Ida. "I know Janice and her family will be fine with you. When the time is right, we'll tell the police. Until then, mum's the word."

It was her turn to nod and send a smile.

CHAPTER THIRTY-FOUR

The next morning was a flurry of activity. When I was a secretary, I wore business clothes. But now, the unflattering denim pants designed for men had become my workday attire. Today would be different. I would be dining with Eleanor Roosevelt.

As I laid out my clothes, I reminded myself this was not a festive visit. I chose my gray silk suit—a jacket and calf-length skirt. I selected my new white ruffled blouse. I'd saved it for a special occasion. What's more special than this, I thought. I slipped on my patent leather pumps and reached for a matching handbag. My flared black Persian lamb coat plus a matching cap sitting jauntily and confident on my head completed the picture.

I checked my appearance in the hall mirror, swirling this way and that. *Zelda the welder was going to lunch at the White House.* I look swell, I thought, winking at my reflection.

Zelda the Welder

At six-thirty sharp, I sat waiting at my front window when I saw an elegant, black car pull up. Heart racing, I kissed Meow, telling him, "There is plenty of food and water for you. Guard our house."

At a knock, I stepped outside and locked the door behind me. I looked over my shoulder and waved to my feline as he stationed himself at his post. The uniformed driver held the car door. I nodded, feeling like a celebrity, and settled into the Cadillac.

This was ordered for me.

The ride to Grand Central Station took less than an hour, not bad for that time of morning. When we arrived, I stepped out of the car and stood transfixed, staring at the magnificent East 42nd Street façade. A clock sat in the center of a large sculpture of Greek and Roman mythology. Figures of Hercules, Mercury, and Minerva stood before me. A fleeting smile touched my face as I remembered them from my school studies. The large hands on the clock's face read seven-twenty. I had a few minutes.

I stepped to the ticket booth and got in line to pick up my pass and return ticket. I glanced nervously at people milling in all directions around me. A twinge of fear surged through my chest.

What if Big Joe found out what I was doing? What if he were in the terminal right now ready to stop me?

I accepted my tickets, slipped them in my purse, and moved on quickly.

The Oyster Bar Restaurant was close by. I found a bench outside and sat where I could see in all directions. I looked at each face as they passed. No one I recognized—yet.

This nonsense has to stop. Relax. I must be ready to speak to Mrs. Roosevelt.

A sign next to the restaurant claimed the spot to be a landmark. It was called the Whispering Gallery. Acoustics transported whispers from one corner of the hall to the other. I imagined the din could be overwhelming with a full house of travelers. People were already filling the station. A thought occurred to me. This could be a good place to scream for help, if it became necessary.

You're acting like a fool. Stop it.

I tried to relax. I let my eyes drift over the area, taking in the expanse, the great size of the hall. Pink marble floors mirrored the morning sunshine breaking through the upper level. Cathedral windows covered with heavy grating were almost as tall as the walls. They looked down on the terminal like sentinels. A line of round light bulbs ran the upper level of the wall, placed to highlight the ceiling—a now-faded fresco of star constellations silhouetted against a no longer bright blue sky. Brilliant when it was new, it now cried for restoration. Time and the accumulation of grime had done their dirty work.

It might be fun painting the heavens like Michelangelo in the Sistine Chapel. I'd rather do that than be at Federal, worried that men wanted my friend dead.

The thought made me realize how tense I was. Everything seemed ominous. Even the stories-high chandeliers seemed to reflect an eerie glow. Voices swarmed, bees filling the hall with a constant humming. I felt small in the openness. I wanted to be on my way. The more I had to wait, the more nervous I became.

Many travelers were servicemen—soldiers, sailors, marines of all stripe and rank. They hurried about, moving from one end of the terminal to the other. Some were home on leave. Some were returning to camp. In their faces I read intensity. Or perhaps it was anxiety.

I surrendered to bedlam, to the ceaseless activity of the teeming building. I glanced at my watch, then at the small shops flanking the sides of the hall. It might be nice to examine their wares. Did I have time?

At that moment, the announcer's voice sang out, "Boarding now for Washington D.C. All aboard."

I got in line and glanced around. Then I froze. Walking from the other end of the hall was a tall, handsome man. He wore a hat. I couldn't make out his features from the distance, but he had the bearing and appearance of Big Joe. He wore a crooked grin as he walked straight toward me. I couldn't move, just stood locked in place, staring as he approached. He reached the line, walked passed me, and took his place beside the woman waiting for him. It wasn't Big Joe. Up close, he looked nothing like Big Joe.

I'm such a fool. How could I be so stupid? Why am I so afraid? What could anyone do to me here?

Zelda the Welder

A young woman stood in line in front of me. She was struggling with an oversized suitcase, pushing it along as the line slowly moved forward.

I would have liked to help, but her luggage would have overwhelmed me, also. I concentrated on her, trying to take my mind off my fears. She was a pretty little thing. What brought her to Grand Central Station? Where was she headed with that huge case? Perhaps she was on her way to visit her guy in the service. That would be nice.

A sailor approached her. He tapped the slender girl on the shoulder, grinning like a small boy when she looked up. His navy uniform fit him like he was born to wear it. His white cap sat cocked at a forty-five degree angle over his very blue eyes. He pointed to the suitcase and said, "Pardon me, ma'am. May I help you with that?"

She nodded, I thought rather shyly. He picked up the case like it was a bag of feathers. Walking beside her, he carried it to the train platform. Placing it on the top step, he bowed and touched the tip of his hat in a salute. She thanked him with a huge grin.

The gallant incident restored my joy in going to Washington. A great bunch of folk lived in the USA. And this was New York. I loved my city. I prayed everything would soon be restored to normal. Life had its rough spots, but it was also full of strange and wonderful things. *I, Zelda Bea, was lunching at the White House. Fancy that.*

I boarded the train. From my window seat, I saw the porter fold up the train steps. I heard a long toot of the whistle and then the clank-clank-clank of metal wheels on metal tracks as we picked up speed. A billow of gray smoke passed my window. The train was on its way.

I had never been on a locomotive before. I peered out the window, fascinated as the scenes flew by. But expectations of what was to come took over as I gathered my thoughts. I hoped my appeal to Mrs. Roosevelt's famous good will would work, that she would find a way to stop the thieves and bring them to justice. We must tell the police—but who could we trust? The longer we waited, the more dangerous the situation became. My greatest fear was that Big Joe or his cohorts would find

Janice before the police caught them. How long could she and her family safely hide in a house across the street from mine? Two days? Three? How long before someone got wise?

The slowing of the train garnered my attention. In little more than three hours, the train stopped at Union Station.

CHAPTER THIRTY-FIVE

Following the crowd, I made my way out of the train station to the busy street. A tall, majestic statue of Christopher Columbus greeted me at the entrance to Union Station. Smaller statues surrounded it. American flags hung on either side of the statue's semi-circular background. The flags enhanced the monument's spectacular appearance. This station's wonderful architecture was every bit as outstanding as that at Grand Central Station. I could enjoy spending the day at either place, shopping and dining and watching the people.

Only not this time.

Parked at the curb in front of me stood the President's personal Cadillac. I regarded the elegant black car bearing the Presidential Seal. My stomach did a little dance.

It waited for me, Zelda Bea.

As I approached, the driver tipped his cap and said, "Miss Bea?"

I nodded. He held the door, and I slid onto the back seat. I smiled. It would be easy to get used to having a liveried chauffeur.

I pushed vanity aside. I must think only of my reason for being here. Janice and her family waited at home. They were holding on, praying for the help I'd promised. Please, let everything go well at the White House.

The drive was short. The car moved around Columbus Circle, down a small street, and on to Pennsylvania Avenue. Gazing out the window, I promised myself that one day when the war was over and life was back to normal I would come to Washington, DC, to visit the memorials and dedications in this great city.

We drove down the long driveway and pulled up to the main entrance of 1600 Pennsylvania Avenue. After helping me from the car, the driver escorted me up a short flight of narrow steps to a massive door.

Missy met me inside the entrance. She looked to be about my age. Her wavy hair was in an upswept do. The buttons of her blouse looked like pearls. I showed her my identification. Smiling, she ushered me to the stately room where Madam Eleanor Roosevelt waited.

The First Lady rose from her chair, arms outstretched to grasp mine. "I am so pleased to see you, my dear. Did you have a pleasant trip?"

"Oh, I did. It was an experience, I must say, visiting the two great stations. A first for me. I didn't know we had anything so grand. And now the White House." I looked up into her pleasant face. I knew my excitement was showing. I tried to relax and not look like a tourist.

A smile eased her features. "I agree. The buildings *are* imposing. But you must be tired. Please sit down and have some tea." She sat, indicating I take the chair across from her, then nodded to the tray and tea service on the table at her side. "Lunch will be ready soon, but first, we must talk. Tell me about the trouble your friend is in."

I took a deep breath and plunged right in, leaving nothing out. Big Joe held center stage with all his disgusting antics. When I described how I hit him with the piece of metal, she gasped then nodded.

"I like your moxie," she said. "You looked fear in the face."

Her gentle smile encouraged me to continue. When I finished, she was silent for several minutes.

Did my story sound contrived?

"Zelda, you say you know two of the people involved in these nasty goings-on. Your foreman, Joe Morgan, the raunchy character. And a man named Hansen."

"Yes. Fen Hansen is the man who runs Kearny Federal."

"Oh?"

"I was surprised, too. Mr. Hansen would be the last person I would suspect. How could the man running the Kearny Federal Shipyard think he would get away with stealing scrap metal from the federal government?"

"He must have thought he was above suspicion. I suppose that is what makes criminals do what they do. Are you certain you don't know who the third man might be?"

I shook my head. "That is the other problem. Janice told me they mentioned a police officer, but she didn't catch his name. She only knew they called him O."

John O'Reilly's face flashed before me. "A detective in New Jersey's Kearny precinct was assigned to find Janice. His name is O'Reilly. You must see why I'm reluctant to tell him I found Janice."

"Yes, I see your dilemma. You did right to come to me. It is not safe for you, either." She was quiet for a moment, then nodded like she had come to a decision. "We must be sure Janice and her family is safe until these heinous people are put away. Yes, I shall go to the FBI. We will let them take it from here. They should make short work of it."

I clasped my fingers together so tightly my arms shook.

She took my hands in hers, patting them gently. "My dear. Will you leave the rest to me?"

I nodded, feeling the weight of fear and concern slipping from my shoulders. My eyes filled with tears as my smile grew. "That's why I called you."

Mrs. Roosevelt stood and picked up the phone from a corner table. After a moment, I heard her say, "Yes, please. I'd like to talk to…" Her voice faded as she paced away. I couldn't catch the name of the person she spoke to or any of her conversation. She nodded several times. Then, the call completed, she replaced the earpiece. "There now, it is done."

There was a tap on the door, and a woman wearing a starched white uniform entered. She spoke softly to the First Lady.

"Ah. Very good. Our lunch is ready," Mrs. Roosevelt said. She beckoned me and put her arm around my shoulder. "Come, my dear."

We walked down the hall to a bright, sunny room. President Roosevelt and Vice President Wallace sat at the table. They stopped their conversation, looking up when we entered. I blinked. My eyes felt like they were popping.

"This is a lovely spot," said Mrs. Roosevelt, one arm sweeping the room majestically. "When we're at home together, we like to have our meals here. We are apart so much, it is nice to find a moment to catch up." She took my hand. "Franklin. Henry. Please meet Zelda Bea, the young lady who saved my life."

The President gave me little more than a surprised grunt. He adjusted his monocle as he looked me up and down.

Mr. Wallace, however, placed his napkin on the table and stood. He tilted his head in a slight bow. "Mrs. Roosevelt… Miss Bea."

I bowed my head in response. "Mr. Roosevelt. Mr. Wallace," I said, feeling giddy being in such prestigious company.

Mrs. Roosevelt's voice picked up a pitch higher. "Remember, I told you about her. She rescued me from falling through the deck into the water. Can you believe this slip of a girl is a welder?"

The Vice President's eyebrows shot up at the mention of my work. His smile grew wide. "Ah, a welder. How interesting. The country is in your debt."

My face felt hot. I was sure it was beet-red.

Once the lady of the house and I were seated, the Vice President sat back down, replacing his napkin on his lap.

My eyes went to the President. I wondered why he had remained seated when we entered. Then I saw the large wheels on either side of his chair. I hadn't known he used a wheelchair all the time. Sometimes when he gave a speech, he appeared to be standing. It was deceptive.

Zelda the Welder

When he looked at me, I cast my eyes down, afraid he would think I was staring.

Get hold of yourself. He's only a man. He just happens to be the President of the United States.

Then he said, "I am very happy to meet you, Miss Bea. Thank you for coming to Eleanor's aid. You did a great service to my family, young lady. We will be eternally grateful for your quick thinking."

"I was happy I was there," I said, my voice no louder than a mouse's squeaks.

I wasn't sure he heard me. He'd gone back to speaking with Mr. Wallace.

We were served vegetable soup in a creamy broth, crispy rolls with butter, and a small green salad.

"This is delicious," I said.

"I'm so glad you're enjoying it," said Mrs. Roosevelt. "The vegetables are from my Victory Garden."

I smiled at her, struck by how down to Earth she seemed.

As we ate, the Vice President said, "Perhaps, Zelda, you can tell us what it's like to be a welder. It must be daunting work for one as… young as you."

The President looked up, then went back to eating his steaming soup.

I set down my spoon. *A simple question. How should I answer?* "Welding is not difficult once you learn how. The hardest part is climbing to the top of a mammoth destroyer escort when you're afraid of heights." I couldn't hold back a wide grin.

I heard a chuckle, and the President chimed in. "I don't think I would like that, either. Terra firma for me."

"Do you feel challenged?" asked Mr. Wallace.

"Absolutely. And terrified," I said. "But more than that, I feel honored to help in the war with our boys fighting overseas. All of us at Federal feel the same."

He said, "I don't know where we'd be without brave women like you stepping up to fill the gap."

I cleared my throat "Mr. Wallace, sir?" The room fell silent as their faces turned my way. I know I blushed. "What are the duties of the Vice President in this time of war? They must be monumental and challenging as well. So much has been happening at once."

Zelda the Welder

"Well, I can't go into everything. Confidential you know, however," and he went into a detailed and possibly fanciful account of a day in his life in Washington.

I gasped and laughed in all the right places. It was fun. I wanted lunch to go on forever. Or at least a while longer. But a man slid through the room and whispered in the President's ear. Immediately, the two men excused themselves.

"Meeting you has been a pleasure," Henry Wallace said, bowing over my hand. "Carry on the good work. Keep building those great warships. We need you out there. Just be careful when you climb."

I beamed. "I enjoyed meeting you both. I will have something to tell my children, someday."

The President's resonant voice bellowed, "Come on, Henry, we've got work to do, too. There *is* a war on, you know." He chuckled like he'd just told a great joke.

I had heard he was austere. I hadn't found him to be gruff, but he did appear to be tired. His face was drawn like he hadn't had much sleep lately.

The table was being cleared. I was sorry to see everything go. It had smelled so good. Tasted so good. I must tell the girls about the Presidential Victory Garden.

Mrs. Roosevelt interrupted my thoughts. "There is still an hour before you have to leave for the train station. What would you like to do?"

I hesitated. "Don't think me foolish, but I'd love to see some of the White House. The parts visitors don't get to see."

"Well then, you shall," she said.

We were on the second floor, and we walked to the room on the southeast corner and on through to another room.

"Abraham Lincoln's office," Mrs. Roosevelt said. She pointed to a table. "Here is where the sixteenth president spent a lot of his time. This suite was also Mr. Lincoln's Cabinet room." She gestured at the four Lincoln Cabinet chairs flanking a desk. "Take a look over there. That is a copy of the Gettysburg Address."

I leaned in to read it, then turned to her. "Those were exceptional times."

"Yes," she said, obviously pleased at my interest. "Impressive, isn't it? He was quite a leader. His vision is rarely matched. It was here President Lincoln signed the Emancipation Proclamation. Right here, on

January 1, 1863. One of five signed, dated, and titled by Lincoln."

"He led the way."

"He did, indeed." She looked at the watch on her wrist. "It's getting on. Let's move to my rooms. We can sit and talk a short while."

We walked to the west wing and entered a room crammed with traditional furnishings. The walls were covered, floor to ceiling, with framed photos. They were all sizes, all of smiling people. I assumed they were of family and friends.

I found a puffed up velvet couch and relaxed into it. Mrs. Roosevelt sat in an armchair close by. We spent the next half hour discussing her vegetable garden and the economy of fruits and vegetables. We didn't mention Janice.

The clock chimed, and I glanced up. "The hour's gone. The time passed so fast."

"As it does when it is enjoyable. We'll talk more next time," she said.

Next time? I hoped that was a promise.

CHAPTER THIRTY-SIX

Reluctantly, I said goodbye to The First Lady. My new friend. As I left the White House, I glanced about, trying to sear it all into memory. I would have liked to stay and see more of this wonderful place so chock full of history. But I had a train to catch.

The trip home went like clockwork. The chauffeur dropped me off at precisely six o'clock. I ran across the street to Ida's house. My friends were just sitting down to dinner, and I happily joined in. Tonight, Ida was serving her prize-worthy Polish stew with pork, red cabbage, and handfuls of mushrooms.

As we gathered around the table, I was bombarded with questions.

"How did it go?" Sadie asked.

"Was the White House beautiful?" Ida said dreamily.

Janice avoided my eyes as if she dreaded the outcome.

Zelda the Welder

I sat at Ida's feast with my elbows on the table, chin on clasped hands, and looked around at my friends. "Settle down and let me tell you of my experiences at the White House. First, I want you to know Mrs. Roosevelt has agreed to help us. She has already put a plan in action."

"Really?" Janice blurted, looking shocked.

"Really." I patted her hand. "You and your family will be safe soon enough."

I glanced about the table, meeting each set of eyes, glad I hadn't broken my promise to them. Sadie grinned broadly and passed around bowls of food.

Little Billy, his fork grasped tightly in one hand, began shoveling Ida's wonderful stew into his tiny mouth. He looked up, cheeks full, head cocked, and leveled his unconcerned eyes on me. Then he went back to the contents on his plate.

I grinned at him, then filled my own plate.

"Go on. Tell us," Ida said.

"I won't forget this day for a long, long time. After our talk about the nasty goings-on as Mrs. R. put it, a servant led us to the Roosevelt's lovely private dining room. Sun flooded the room from three long, narrow windows. The light fell on the two gentlemen sitting at the table." I couldn't hold back a chuckle before I put on a sober face.

"So, who was it?" Ida asked.

I forked in a bite of pork and chewed a moment, savoring the flavor. Their impatient faces made me grin. As I spoke each name, I paused to watch their expressions. "Vice President Wallace... and..." I made the sound of a drumroll. "President Roosevelt, himself."

An audible NO resounded around the dining table. Ida and Sadie's questions flew at me—What did they say? How did they act? What did they wear?

"They stopped their conversation when we walked in. Mr. Wallace stood and addressed us with a smile and a nod. He was quite charming."

"What did the President do?" Ida said.

"I wondered why he didn't stand as well. But he wasn't being impolite. He was in a wheelchair. He looked up, wearing that monocle of his and his famous smile. His eyes moved to me. I was embarrassed I'd been caught staring, and I averted my eyes. I felt my face flush. Wasn't that childish of me?"

Ida and Sadie were engrossed in the tale. They raised serious faces, nodding. I *had* been silly.

I tried to make my voice high-pitched in order to imitate the famous lady. "Franklin, Henry, I'd like you to meet Zelda Bea, the young lady who saved my life. After which, she smiled that warm, wide smile of hers."

"Ooh," said Sadie.

"Ah," said Ida.

Imitating the President's voice was more difficult, but I worked at it. "I am very happy to meet you, Miss Bea. Thank you for coming to Eleanor's aid. He adjusted his monocle over his aristocratic nose. May I call you Zelda? he said, and without waiting for my answer, went on. You did a great service to my family, young lady. We will be eternally grateful for your quick thinking. With that, he held the pose and the smile for a moment longer, and before I could get in a single word, he turned back to complete his quiet conversation with Mr. Wallace."

"Well," Ida said, "I don't know if I like that. After thanking you for saving his wife's life, he dismisses you?"

"Oh, Ida, it wasn't like that. We had most likely interrupted some important business. After a moment, they joined our conversation, Mrs. R. leading the party. She indicated I was to sit next to her. A servant held our chairs, first hers, then mine."

"What did you eat?" asked Ida.

"Bowls of steaming vegetable soup were set at our places, and a soup urn placed on the table. There were warm rolls and butter on the table—real butter, Ida. There was also a vegetable salad, and fruit—all from their Victory Garden. They grow enough that they don't have to worry about rations at the White House, and they donate quite a lot to the needy. I had heard that Mrs. R. was frugal, what with the war and all. But what we had was sufficient and good. I was thrilled to sit at their table.

"Mr. Wallace questioned me about Federal, the work we do there, the ships, what it is like to be a welder. I told him of my climbing a ladder on the outside of a huge ship to reach the top deck. He wanted to know if I felt challenged. Absolutely, I told him, and terrified. The President laughed at that." I turned to Janice, trying to get her into the conversation. "He must fear heights, too, don't you think?"

She shifted in her chair as if uncomfortable.

I became serious. "I told them how honored I felt to help in the war with our boys fighting overseas. That all of us at Federal felt the same. I didn't get into what I was there for, why I was seeing Mrs. Roosevelt, and they didn't ask. Perhaps the President thought I was invited because I had helped his wife. I figured, if Mrs. R. wanted them to know why I was really there, she would tell them in her own good time.

"After lunch, we talked a while longer. I told them that I had friends in the service, and I worried about them, about all the men fighting overseas. I hoped the war would be over soon, that all our boys would come home safely. The President said with two fronts it would be a bit longer than if we had only Germany to contend with. I know they tried to keep it low-keyed. It wouldn't do to tell a civilian like me too much. But I was glad to be there, to put my thoughts out." I sighed. "Imagine. I was having an intelligent conversation with the President and the Vice President, not to mention our very clever First Lady. After about twenty minutes of this conversation the President's secretary came into the room. Mr. Wallace stood. After his courteous, Carry on the good work, Keep building our great ships, It was a pleasure meeting you... I was glowing. Then he and the President left."

"Is he in a wheelchair all the time, our President?" Sadie asked.

"He'd rather it wasn't known, and Mrs. R. asked me not to mention it, so please, just between us. After the men left, Mrs. R. and I did some sightseeing. It's a lovely old building. So many great people have lived there, so many ghosts. Eleanor Roosevelt is a truly sincere person. We talked about many things. Finally the driver arrived to drive me to the train." I smiled at Janice, willing her to speak.

"What did she say about me?" Janice asked.

She *was* taking an interest. For a while she had seemed lost in some other world. "That I must tell you not to worry, everything was being taken care of. She wouldn't say more than that they will let us know when the men are in custody and you are safe to go about your business. It shouldn't take long," I added, attempting to bring some glow back to her face.

Janice nodded, her chair creaking as she shifted her thin body. For the first time since I got home, I looked at her closely. The overlarge, gray sweater she'd borrowed from Ida brought no color to her face. Her usually sparkling eyes looked dull. This wasn't my friend, Janice the Charmer, the lovely girl who didn't have to do anything but look at the boys to attract them. And she wasn't eating, just pushing her food around on her plate. The weak smile on her face didn't go any farther than her lips. The whole mess had taken its toll. Perhaps a professional could help her deal with the past days.

Billy carefully lifted a glass of milk with two chubby hands then drank it down thirstily. The napkin tucked under his chin caught the dribbles. I worried for him, for Sadie, for Janice, for the threat they still faced, but I had done all I could. I'd vowed to leave it in Mrs. Roosevelt's hands.

Now, I had to get some sleep. I'd spent a day I'd never forget. But thrilling as it was, I was exhausted. I stood. "Ida, I must beg off helping you clean up. It will be my turn tomorrow, I promise."

"Off with you," Ida said. "I have enough willing hands. Good night, famous lady."

I looked at the group sitting around the table. I loved them all. "Goodnight." I turned to Billy. "How about a big hug for me?" I whispered in his tiny ear, "And give Mom an extra big one, okay?"

He tilted his head back. With an earnest stare, he nodded. A mustache of milk decorated his face. My heart did a flip-flop for this sweet little boy. *Please keep him safe* was the theme running through my thoughts.

Outside, I stepped around yesterday's piled-up snow, and carefully walked across the road. The blacktop shone in the moonlight, all melted and wet and clean looking.

I stopped and stared. Detective O'Reilly's car sat parked in front of my house. His car door opened, and he stepped out. A chill ran down my spine.

"Good news or bad news?" I asked.

"Which would you prefer?" he said.

"No stupid questions," I muttered and unlocked my door.

Meow, purring softly, jumped off his perch at the window. He rubbed against my leg, then leapt into O'Reilly's arms, where he sat, cradled.

I gave my pet a sidelong glance, and took a deep breath. "Well, hello, Meow. It's nice to see you, too." I walked into the living room.

The detective followed, rubbing his hand down Meow's back. "I understand you found Janice Bates."

"I understand you didn't."

"It's like that, is it?"

"What are you doing here? Are you following me?" I said, not sure whether I should be angry or frightened. Was he a good guy or a bad guy? I still didn't know.

"Just arrived. I wanted to tell you the good news."

I felt my face grow hot. "Really? Is it customary to drive all the way to Long Island when a phone call would do?"

"Miss Bea, the FBI was in touch with me this afternoon. They wanted all I knew about the Bates case. It was over in short order. We have all three perpetrators. Caught them cold. They were packing scrap metal into a truck behind that house you took me to. They won't be able to squirm out of it."

My mouth dropped open. For a moment, I could only stare at him. *Over? It was over?* "I know about Joe and Fen. Who was the third party? O, I think they called him."

"Fen Hansen, the manager, set it up. Joe Morgan was the muscle man. And Otto Klein was the inside man."

"Otto-the-cop?"

"He had all the information they needed, where and when the trucks got in, what they carried, that sort of thing. Klein quaked when we caught him. Told all. The three had already banked a handsome profit selling stolen scrap metal to the enemy. That's treason in a time of war."

"They found them so quickly."

"When you go over someone's head, you don't fool around." He flashed me a smile. "It must be nice to know people in high places. I wouldn't mind having Madam Eleanor Roosevelt on my side."

"All you have to do is save her life," I murmured under my breath. At his perplexed expression, I cleared my throat and said, "Would you like some coffee?"

"No, thank you. I just wanted you to know you and your friends can feel safe now. I'll want to see you and Janice Bates at my office in the morning. I have some questions for her. I hope she'll agree to press charges. And I want a report from you. All of it this time. Then you're free to pick up your lives again."

"Thank you, Detective. I will sleep better tonight."

He put Meow down and walked to the door, turned, looked at me, seemed about to say something, didn't, and then continued outside to his car. The motor started.

"Bye," I said. My eyes followed his car as it turned and left my street.

When he was gone, I returned to Ida's house. I knocked quietly.

Ida answered the door. "Shh. Billy's asleep on the couch."

"I need to speak to Janice for a moment," I whispered. "Can she come out here?"

Ida nodded and closed the door partway as she stepped back inside.

A moment later, Janice appeared. "What's happened?"

I took her hands in mine. "They got them. All three men are in police custody."

She gasped. "Are you sure?"

"And you'll never guess who O was. Otto."

She stared blankly. "Otto? The cop?"

She began to laugh—great barking guffaws that slowly dissolved into tears. She clung to me, her sobs becoming more and more hysterical. All I could do was hold her, knowing my Janice would never be the same.

CHAPTER THIRTY-SEVEN

Since it was Saturday, I allowed myself the luxury of lying in bed for a few extra minutes. I wasn't looking forward to going to the stationhouse today. I didn't think Janice was up to a police interrogation.

But when I knocked on Ida's door, Janice was dressed and ready. We said our goodbyes to the others then got into my car. Janice didn't say much as we drove along. Mostly she just gazed out the window at the passing billboards.

Finally, she said, "Everything looks the same."

"What do you mean?"

"It looks the same as before."

"Life goes on." I nodded. "Look, you have every right to be sad and angry and confused. You didn't deserve what they did to you. But it's in the past. You were stronger than they knew, and you lived through it."

"Because of you."

"All I did was find you." I glanced at her. *"You survived."*

She nodded and fell silent. Several minutes passed. Then she said, "Ida has talked us into staying with her for the rest of the weekend. She and my mother have become fast friends."

"Then you'll go home on Monday?"

"I've decided to go to work on Monday."

"So soon? Are you sure you're up to it?"

"I think so," she said. "Besides, I've been gone for over a week. Someone has to bring home the bacon."

I smiled. "It will be good to have you. But I'm not climbing any ladders."

She laughed. "No. I'm keeping my feet firmly on the ground."

By the time we got to Kearny, the parking lot in front of the police station was packed with personnel coming and going. We parked in the visitors' area and walked to the front door. As we entered, Detective O'Reilly walked toward us. A broad smile lit his face. Evidently, he'd been watching for us. Seeing him again gave me a warm feeling in the pit of my stomach.

He inclined his head. "Miss Bea. Miss Bates. Thank you for coming in this morning. This way."

We zigzagged through the room to his desk. He pulled an extra chair around, and Janice and I sat.

He looked at us from across his desk. "First, I have to tell you that I cannot offer you gas stamps to recompense you for the gas you used in driving here from Long Island."

I huffed out a breath and rolled my eyes.

"You have to demand it," he said. "You have to chastise me."

"Very well," I said. "I demand that you give me gas stamps. It was a two-hour drive to get here. I chastise you."

"I stand chastised." He lowered his eyes. Then he opened a folder and slid a voucher my way.

I sniffed, trying to keep the humor from my voice. "Well, it won't fill my tank."

He gave me one of his blinding smiles. I sighed. *He was damned good looking.* I swallowed my thoughts. This was about Janice.

Detective O'Reilly sobered. "Miss Bates, I know you've been through a lot, and I'm sorry to have to ask you to relive it all for me. The more information we have, the stronger our case will be against these men. I'm going to take you into a quiet room, just the two of us. There will be a tape recorder. Just answer my questions."

Janice nodded, avoiding his eyes.

"The good part is that you can have as much coffee as you like," he said. "And there should still be doughnuts, if you want one."

"Coffee is fine," she said with a faint smile.

"Should I wait here?" I asked.

"Yes," he said. "I've asked Eddie to take your statement. Tell him *everything*."

"Even about my trip to the White House?"

He blinked at me, looking surprised and then exasperated. "You can summarize that part."

He stood and ushered Janice away. As he passed, I touched his arm.

"I want to ask you to be gentle with her," I said quietly. "When I found her she was ready to break."

Zelda the Welder

He nodded. "I'll try to make it as quick and painless as I can."

When he left, Officer Edward Tully joined me. He didn't have to prod me with questions. I walked him through what had happened step by step leaving nothing out. Then he typed up the report, and I signed it.

Two cups of coffee later, I saw Janice and O'Reilly approaching. I got to my feet.

"See?" he told me. "Not so bad."

"Detective O'Reilly, you *have* been helpful. And I haven't always been all that sweet about it." I smiled sheepishly. "Forgive me, and thank you."

"May I ask you something?"

"Yes?"

He looked directly at me, his eyes never wavering from mine. "Would you care to have dinner with me tonight? I can pick you up at home."

I was surprised and not surprised. I was pleased. I was confused. What to say to this tall, handsome man who didn't mind driving two hours for a date with me? And what would be the harm in being friends? "Thank you. I'd like that. Would eight o'clock be all right?"

"Sounds like a plan. I'll see you then." He winked. "And call me John."

Monday morning came fast. Jimmy pulled up to my door. Mary sat next to him on the passenger side, and Annie sat in the back.

When Janice and I stepped out of my house, I saw their expressions change. Even before we slid into the backseat, their questions flew at us. They wanted to know everything.

"Janice," Annie shouted. "Are you all right?"

"Where were you?" Mary cried.

"She was in that house, just like we thought," I told her. "Big Joe had her tied up in the cellar."

A few choice words for Big Joe floated in the air. Hey, they were letting off steam. It had been a long, worrying time. While we covered the miles to New Jersey, I reiterated the last few days.

"When I told Eleanor Roosevelt our story, she called in the FBI. We have her to thank. She's a wonderful woman. Now Big

Joe Morgan, Fen Hanson, and Otto are in jail, caught red-handed. Stupid them. Best part, Janice is safe." I turned to her. "Right?"

Mary said, "Of course."

"Oh, yes," Annie said.

"Thanks, girls." Janice looked at me. "I really have you, Zelda, to thank for my life. I couldn't have gone on much longer. I really thought I was going to die." She turned her eyes back to the girls. "And then Zelda was there. You had to see her. She gave Big Joe a wham, and he was out." Janice beamed at me, and the girls turned my way, faces lit as they stared.

I blushed. "I only did what anyone would do."

Mary let out a yell. "No, you did a whole lot more. You never gave up. And you, Janice. You broke up a smuggling ring. You deserve a medal."

I smiled, thinking that was what my friend, Eleanor, said when I spoke to her last night.

Mary bounced, turning in her front seat and bending over the back to hug me, then stretching her short body to reach Janice. Then it was Annie's turn. It was easier for her, sitting next to us. A lot of hugging went on.

I sat back and held my ears as the car echoed with squeals of happiness. I saw Jimmy through the rearview mirror. He grinned so hard I thought his face would break.

When everyone calmed down, I told them all about my trip to the White House. I left nothing out—the train ride, the never-to-forget luncheon with Eleanor Roosevelt, the President and Vice President. I even went into the wonderful food from the First Lady's own victory garden. You could say I was bragging, just a bit.

The questions made the time fly, and before we knew it we were in the town of Kearny and pulling through the gates of the shipyard. We arrived fifteen minutes before eight.

I was impatient now to get inside. I wanted to find out what was being said around the Yard about the arrests. I took Janice's arm, then reported for work as I had for the last six months. Only, today I felt a kind of jubilation. There was no Otto-the-cop sneering at us. There was no Big Joe to make me feel small. I felt like I had on the first day I had arrived at Federal. Like the world was opening up. My life had moved on.

The concrete walk stretched before me. Swaying in their locks were the tall ships, finished or still to be finished. Around them was the bustling activity I'd come to know. On my right, busy workers prepared a mighty destroyer for launching. It rocked, waiting to be off as the dark river water sloshed beneath its keel.

Across the walk, a destroyer escort waited. Workers up top were finishing the vessel for its maiden voyage. Against its side leaned a tall, slender ladder. It reached to the top deck. As she climbed it, a welder dragged an electrical line behind her.

The past followed her all the way to the top as my mind watched *me* climbing. Was it only a few days ago? Time moves on, impartial to the consequences.

Several other warships rocked in their slips, waiting to begin their missions, impatient to slide into the brackish water, to leave the Hackensack River, to sail across a blue ocean. To be there for our men, fighting in a nasty war.

I saw waves breaking, whitecaps

foaming. The river stretched far out into the distance, there to meet up with the sea. The cold wind chilled me, but I could handle it. Everything would be all right now.

I bent and picked up my bucket of rods, reached for my torch, and adjusted my shield. We women welders had a war to win.

Federal Shipbuilding and Dry-Dock Co.
Kearny, NJ

Etching by John Taylor Arms, 1943
Commission of United States Navy
Bureau of Ships

Made in the USA
Middletown, DE
13 August 2017